W9-BHR-666

SPY FORCE

mission:
Spy Force Revealed

SPY FORCE

mission:
Spy Force Revealed

BY DEBORAH ABELA · ILLUSTRATED BY GEORGE O'CONNOR

A Paula Wiseman Book · Simon & Schuster Books for Young Readers
New York London Toronto Sydney

Look for all of the

SPY FORCE

adventures

>Mission: In Search of the Time and Space Machine

>Mission: Spy Force Revealed

Coming soon

>Mission: The Nightmare Vortex

>Mission: Hollywood

>Mission: The Amazon Experiment

>Mission: Blue's Revenge

For Todd

SIMON & SCHUSTER BOOKS FOR YOUNG READERS
An imprint of Simon & Schuster Children's Publishing Division
1230 Avenue of the Americas, New York, New York 10020

First published in Australia in 2002 by Random House Australia Pty Ltd
Published by arrangement with Random House Australia Pty Ltd
First illustrated U.S. edition, 2005

Book design by Lucy Ruth Cummins
The text for this book is set in Goudy.
The illustrations for this book are rendered in ink.
Manufactured in the United States of America
10 9 8 7 6 5 4 3 2 1
CIP data for this book is available from the Library of Congress.
ISBN 0-689-87358-1

A LETTER FROM **MAX REMY**, SUPERSPY

Okay, listen. I'm only going to say this once. Just in case you missed what happened last time. My name is Max Remy. I'm eleven, and I live with my busy mother while my dad is a famous film director who lives in California with his young actress wife. I hate school, especially the slime-brained Toby Jennings, who enjoys making my life a complete misery. To get away from him and the other jerks I have to share this planet with, I've invented Alex Crane, a secret spy who works for the international intelligence agency called Spy Force.

The whole story started when I was parceled off to the country last summer to stay with my aunt Eleanor and uncle Ben on their farm. But when I got there, they weren't the chicken farmers I thought they were, but world-famous scientists working on a Time and Space Machine! Trouble was, to finish the machine, Ben needed to find his brother, Francis, whom he hadn't spoken to in years because of a fight they had while working together in London.

With my new friend Linden, I used the machine to travel to England, where we found Ben's brother but also met this evil guy, Mr. Blue, who wanted to steal the Time and Space Machine for himself to use as part of his sinister scheme to rule the world. Soon, though, we ruined his plans and saved humanity from certain doom.

But guess what? When we arrived back home, we got a telegram from Spy Force thanking us for our bravery. From Spy Force! And I thought I'd just made them up.

Anyway, that's all I have to tell you. For other details, you'll just have to read my first story.

Now, let's get on with it.

Max Remy

CHAPTER 1

An Evil Plan and a List of Suspects

Chronicles of Spy Force:

Alex Crane looked out the open exit of the small twin-engine plane as it swooped above the dense treetops of the Amazon jungle. The thick canopy of green hurtled beneath them like an enormous ocean, each treetop another wave in a vast flurry that seemed to last forever. They were flying so close Alex was sure that if she ran a hand along the leaves, she could have scooped up the dew that was sprinkled over the jungle like a giant handful of liquid gold. She fixed her eyes on the landscape below and thought to herself, whoever was responsible for making the world was showing off when they made this part.

Suddenly the plane lurched sideways as it struck a pocket of turbulence. Alex's head hit the cold metal wall with a thud as the giant of a man who was in charge of the mission launched another tirade against the pilot.

"Where'd you get your license from? The back of a cereal box? My three-year-old nephew could fly this plane better than you. They've trained chimps that could outdo your aviation skills."

Alex was impressed. She'd been dealing with Blue's thugs for years, and *aviation* was the longest word she'd ever heard from any of them.

The pilot's face remained unchanged. He'd heard all about this guy from the other pilots and had already filled his ears with cotton wool so that none of his cursing could filter through.

The suited tough adjusted his seat belt tighter around his waist before pulling out a floral handkerchief and wiping his brow. The short, fat guy sitting next to him stared.

"Floral?" he smirked.

"It was a present from my daughter." The tough guy said it like a warning, his nerves making him more edgy than usual.

He'd been nervous since the trip began and if Alex's guess was right, the pilot was as skilled as they came and was getting great pleasure out of the occasional and "unexpected" turbulence the plane was experiencing.

Just then, the short, fat guy buried his head in his lap and filled another sickbag with vomit. Alex thought she saw the faintest of grins on the pilot's face.

She adjusted the miniature parachute on her back and crawled across the metal floor of the cargo plane between wooden crates that were stacked like bowling pins. Taking out her laser knife, she carefully broke the reinforced seals on a few of the crates before she found it. A small humidifier case that, if she was right, was packed with exactly what she was looking for, and it was her job to get her hands on it before the case reached Blue.

Alex had boarded the plane in a village called Manaus on the banks of the Amazon River. Well, not quite "boarded." She "snuck on" while Mr. Blue's thugs were busy working out new ways to yell at the locals who were about to fly them into the jungle's deep and mysterious heart. On top of their fear of flying, the thugs were also nervous about their destination. It was said that the natives had cursed the area, so that any outsider who entered was doomed. Stories had been told of only three known attempts to defy the curse and how each of the trespassers had been struck down by a hideous rash that slowly encrusted their skin before they slipped into a deep and fatal coma.

Alex was taking a big risk going on this mission, but it was a risk worth taking in order to thwart Blue's latest villainous operation. Blue had heard about an ancient plant that grew in the Amazon and had remained secret for thousands of years except to a few locals. The *Tropaeolum majorium*, or Fire of Life, was a small, innocent-looking plant with a large orange flower that, when combined with a few other green leafy fronds and put through a precise fermentation process, produced an elixir to preserve life for eternity. A veritable fountain of youth. The locals who drank it had been alive for hundreds of years but no one looked over thirty years old. Anyone with half a brain, even a quarter of a brain with slight malfunctions, would know that the potion would revolutionize the world, but would also lead to massive overpopulation and, what's worse, having to put up with Blue longer than any planet could bear.

After finding out about the plant by some sneaky, covert scheming, Blue tricked a few locals into selling him the plant, paying them a fraction of what he stood to make. He also made a few grand promises he had no intention of honoring once he'd got what he wanted.

Thump! The plane hit another air pocket as Alex carefully took the humidifying case from its crate. She knew she was holding something precious, something nature and history had protected for centuries, and that if Blue got his hands on it, the very future of the planet was in jeopardy. She looked through the small, glass window in the side of the case and saw it: the leaves and the orange flower. She had to succeed.

The plane hummed beneath them as she carefully placed the case in her backpack, secured the straps, and crawled back to the exit hatch at the side of the plane. Checking her parachute one more time, she readied herself to unhook the rope that was strung across the exit, when the plane struck another jolt of turbulence. Alex lost her grip and was flung into the aisle of the plane in full view of Blue's thugs. Their eyes only just managed to stay in their sockets. First from fear and then from the shock of seeing her.

The bigger thug looked at the crates and saw they'd been tampered with. His eyes then slowly moved toward Alex like a shark silently swimming toward its next meal.

"I think you might have something that belongs to

us," he said in a voice dripping with quiet menace.

Alex sprang toward the exit and in one smooth move, unhooked the rope. She stood on the edge, said a small prayer, and jumped. But as she did, a strap on her backpack caught on a metal railing, leaving her dangling high above the trees. If she fell, it would mean certain and messy doom.

The thug moved toward her like she was an annoying insect he was about to crush. A smile crept onto his lips. Alex struggled to release the strap, but it was no good; with all her weight hanging from her backpack, she'd never succeed.

The thug curled one arm around the metal railing while the other held a knife ready to cut Alex free from the backpack and from the living world, leaving the plant to become the unfortunate property of Blue. He worked the blade across the straps as Alex looked down at her feet waving above the jungle and contemplated her possible last moments of life. Just then one strap was cut. Her body was flung sideways through the air and slammed into the plane. A small blue package jolted free from her pocket and silently grew smaller beneath her as it disappeared into the jungle. The thug, despite his fear of heights, laughed a measly, itchy laugh.

"Bye-bye, Ms. Crane. I doubt even you could save yourself this time."

Is this the end of Alex Crane? Will she free herself

from the plane and Blue's thugs? Will she be able to save the *Tropaeolum majorium*? Will she escape in time to . . .

"Aow!"

Max rubbed the spot on her head where the small blue box crashed into it. It lay a few inches beyond her feet and was no doubt flung at her by some giant bonehead with nothing better to do with his intelligence than prove to the world he didn't have any. She looked at the box and read the message on the side: "Personality delivery for Max Remy." She rolled her eyes. It was a wonder the entire school didn't self-combust from an overload of funny—not!—humor.

Max scanned the school playground to see who the culprit might be.

Suspects No. 1, 2, and 3: Anthony, Richard, and Andy. Also known as the Three Stinkos, not because they smelled, even though that was up for debate, but because they once set off a stink bomb during assembly when Veronica Preston was receiving her "Oh, You Are So Great at Everything Award." (Or something like that.) It was pretty funny, except the whole school had to stand in the hot sun as the stink got worse and listen to the principal lecture them on why the world would be a better place if they all liked each other. Why do adults do that when they know kids hate it?

Suspect No. 4: Russell Allen, or Suss Russ. He was a bit of a loner who spent a lot of his time doing weird things like arranging small pebbles on the ground to look like famous musicians. He'd then call kids over and say, "Guess which rock star that is." Some people said he collected other strange things too, like shoelaces, and that he even had one from some dead prime minister from the 1920s. Weird.

Suspects No. 5 and 6: Antonia Balldalucia and Brigita Stevenson. Max knew they didn't like her since she had accidentally spilled her chocolate milk all over them on the bus one hot afternoon. They never believed it wasn't deliberate no matter how many times she told them. They just glared at her as the milk spread into long brown stains on their uniforms and looked oddly like a map of Italy. After the forty-minute bus trip, the maps had curdled and their walk home was accompanied by the cries of hungry cats. Max spent most of her time trying to avoid standing near them while she was holding any kind of liquid.

Prime suspects: Toby Jennings and Co. There they were sitting on the steps of the main hall like they owned the place. All they needed were a few suits worn over some fat stomachs and they would have resembled overstuffed businessmen carving up the world like a Sunday roast. The first time she'd met them, she'd just arrived at

Hollingdale (Max's third new school in five years), and she made the mistake of accepting an apple they had offered her. She thought they were just trying to be nice but when she took a bite, her teeth sank into the middle of a plump, unsuspecting, and cleverly placed worm. Toby and his pals had dug a long, thin hole into the apple, slid the worm in, and corked it up with a small piece of the fruit. Max had to rinse her mouth out for one hour with Mr. Fayoud's mouthwash before she started feeling normal again. Sometimes, out of nowhere, she still got the taste of worm in her mouth. These suspects were definitely not to be trusted. Ever.

Other suspects: The rest of the playground.

Max's shoulders slumped. Anybody could have thrown the box.

Just then the bell chimed its awful shopping center drone. Like Tinkerbell caught in a time warp. Ms. Peasley, the principal, had it installed rather than a clanging bell because she said it fostered a more harmonious school environment. She actually said that! Where do these people get these ideas? It might as well have been signaling the end of civilization, Max thought, as she prepared to face another two hours with some of the world's undiscovered animal kingdom.

After she'd packed away her lunchbox, she picked up the small blue box and tossed it in the closest garbage can before going to class.

CHAPTER 2

A Mysterious Guest and an Official Invitation

From: Max Remy

To: lindenfranklin@loonmail.com

Subject: Things

Dear Linden,

Just got your e-mail. Thanks! Everything here is pretty normal . . . normal for my life, anyway. Toby topped the class again in science yesterday and you'd think he'd just won the Nobel Prize the way Mrs. Grimshore was going on about it. Dad is still making that big film in LA. And get this! He was having lunch the other day when he met Steven Spielberg. He said he's a nice guy too. Dad doesn't get a lot of time to answer my e-mail, but that's okay. He's always really busy. He sent me this great top that I'm wearing now. He has the best taste. Mom got this promotion, which means she's even more manic than ever, so most of the time she hardly even notices I'm here. Oh, and she's got this new obsession with wheatgrass. Every morning she grinds up this bunch of green grass and makes us both drink it. I'm not kidding. She grows it on the windowsill and it looks just like normal grass. I'm not sure what she thinks it's going to do apart from make me gag and sprout small saplings from my tongue. She said she read that it will make us live longer or get younger or something. I'll just ride this fad out until she finds another one. But she'd better make it quick. I don't know how much more paddock food I can stomach.

"Max, honey. It's time for dinner."

Great! The food guru has just called. Maybe if I stay quiet, she'll forget I'm here. She's good at that. I've written another Alex adventure I'll attach. See what you think. She is on assignment in the Amazon. Why can't my life be like hers? Do you think Spy Force will ever contact us again? I still keep the telegram they sent us in my pocket. Mom put it through the wash once so it looks a little crumpled, but you can still read it.

"Max, sweetie? Did you hear me? Dinner is on the table."

Max sighed and stopped typing.

"Coming!"

Sorry, Linden, gotta go. Super Mom is calling. I'll talk to you tomorrow. Say hello to Ben and Eleanor for me.

Max paused as she tried to think of a way to sign off. She decided to keep it simple.

From Max

She logged off and shut down the computer. She

missed Linden. He was the only one who could make her laugh. Even if his jokes were dumb. Before she met him she was happy not having any friends. She'd made heaps before but just when she was happy, her mom and dad would decide to move again and she had to say good-bye to them, so it was easier not to make any in the first place. But with Linden, it was different. She didn't have to see him all the time to know they were good friends.

She leaned into the cactus on her desk.

"Think yourself lucky you're not a human and you don't have a mother making your life miserable."

Max stood up and opened the door onto the landing at the top of the stairs. She stopped when she heard voices coming from the kitchen. There was her mother's voice talking at a million miles an hour like she normally did, and someone else. A man. Her mom never mentioned anyone coming to dinner and she hadn't heard the doorbell ring either. He must have come home with her. Why didn't her mother get that she liked to be warned when someone else was going to be here? Was that too much to ask?

She tiptoed down the stairs, listening hard and trying to work out who the man was. She crouched low and put her ear against the kitchen door. Her mom was going on about some new show that was starting on TV and how it was going to stop the world, blah blah blah, and whoever the mystery man was, was agreeing with her like she was telling him the secret of life no one had ever stumbled on before.

This was going to be too much. If Max had to sit in a room listening to this all night she was sure she was going to explode. She wouldn't be able to stop it. Then her mom would be sorry.

Just as she was turning around to creep back up the stairs, the kitchen door swung open and her mother only just stopped herself from tripping over Max's crouching body. What she didn't stop was her glass of red wine from spilling all over Max.

"What on earth are you doing on the floor? Didn't you hear me call you for dinner? And look at your new shirt. How am I ever going to get that stain out?"

Now, this scenario could have run a few ways. Some mothers, distraught that they had almost trampled their only beloved child, would have bent down and kissed the child repeatedly as they became overwhelmed by the near-fatal tragedy. Others may have swept their precious daughter snugly into their arms while they apologized for ruining a brand-new shirt that had been given to them as a present. And others may have just felt really bad as they offered a simple and quiet apology.

None of these ever happened in Max's house.

Max's mother looked down at her shirt and only just managed to hold back a blood-curdling scream when she saw that it was totally ruined.

Then her mother remembered she had a guest.

"There's someone in the kitchen I'd like you to meet,"

she said, suddenly sounding all bright.

"Now?" Max was horrified. How could her mother even think of her meeting anyone when she was dripping with wine?

A head appeared from behind the door.

"Hi. I'm Aidan. I've heard heaps about you, Maxine."

Anyone clever enough would see there were a few problems here. First, no one, but no one, ever called her Maxine. That is one of those really important laws of nature you must never forget, like, "Remember to breathe or you will die."

Also, as he made this monumental error against nature, he held out his hand. Max lowered her eyelids to give him a half-eye stare. She'd never heard about this Maxine-calling nobody before and she certainly wasn't about to make physical contact with him. He looked away awkwardly as his hand slowly made its way to a pocket for safety.

Aidan? I've never heard of any Aidan, she thought. And how come he knows about me? Because from his bad clothes and the fact that he's about thirty years younger than my mother, I know all I want to know about him.

There was an uncomfortable pause as nobody knew what to say. A trickle of red wine dribbled from Max's head down her face, adding another stain to her shirt.

"I'm going to get changed," she said.

"Well, don't be long, sweetheart," Max's mom said

with a nervous giggle. "Dinner's getting cold."

If Max had been given a choice of being banished to the coldest regions of Siberia or facing a dinner with her mother and whoever this Aidan was, she'd have known what would have been worse. But since Siberia was out of the question, she changed her clothes and made her way back downstairs.

"Aah, there you are," said her mom in a sickly sweet voice that was like having your head dunked in a barrel of honey. "I've kept your dinner warm for you."

Sweet voice, nice gestures. Max wanted to know where her real mother was.

There was another awkward pause as her dinner was placed in front of her.

"So how was school today?"

Now she really knew this wasn't her mother. She never asked about school.

"Fine," she said, trying to eat as fast as possible so she could escape to somewhere saner.

Awkward pause number three. This meal was going to be worse than Max thought. The ticking of the clock above the fridge got louder and louder.

"Well," said her mother, which never meant good news for Max. "I thought it was about time you and Aidan got to meet."

Her mother looked at her like it was Max's turn to speak but she didn't know what to say, so she kept eating instead.

"Aidan is my boyfriend."

Max dropped her fork sending bits of spaghetti worming all over her lap. Boyfriend? *What boyfriend*, she thought. I've never heard Mom mention a boyfriend before. When did all this happen? People her age don't have boyfriends. They're too old for that kind of thing.

Max was picking spaghetti strands from her lap and wondering why the world just got so crazy. Her mom continued talking.

"So I thought it would be good if you two got to know each other."

You know those times when everything seems to stand still and every second passes like it's an hour? When you want to jump up and get out of where you are but you're stuck and it seems like you'll be there forever? This was one of those times.

"I've got homework to do," said Max as she wiped her mouth on her napkin and stood up.

As she closed the kitchen door behind her, she heard her mother say, "I think that went quite well, don't you?"

That's how it was with her mother. Everything was measured as having gone well or badly. She thought most of what Max did was bad and if things went her way, then everything was going well. It was at times like this when Max missed her dad more than anything.

Upstairs, Max closed her bedroom door, changed into

her pajamas and prepared to stay there all night. E-mailing Linden or writing another Alex Crane adventure would make her feel better. She turned on her computer and discovered she'd received an unusual e-mail. It was marked Top Secret and came with a list of instructions and questions before she could open it.

SECURE FILE

The following e-mail is to be opened by M. Remy. Any person other than M. Remy found to have accessed this file will be subject to the full force of the Protection of Privacy Laws Act of 1926.

Please answer the following security questions before the attached e-mail can be opened:
Name?
Date of Birth?
Address?
First names of only uncle and aunt?

If the questions are answered correctly, you will receive the accompanying mail. Failure to answer the questions correctly or within two minutes will lead to the neutralization of this message.

Linden, thought Max. He was always joking and mostly

this annoyed her, but after what had happened downstairs, she needed all the cheering up she could get. Max answered the questions and hit *send*. She waited eagerly for his reply, but instead, something strange happened to her computer. A series of numbers and letters hurtled up the screen like bugs caught in a wind tunnel. Finally the bugs stopped and the screen went blank.

Max stared at her computer, not knowing what to do next when the following words appeared:

SECURITY CLEARANCE GRANTED.

E-MAIL TO FOLLOW.

Max knew Linden was clever with computers, but she'd never seen him do anything like this before. After two minutes exactly, the e-mail alert appeared before her. Max moved the mouse across the pad and opened it.

From: R. R. Steinberger

To: maxremy@email.com

Subject: Meeting

Dear Max,

This is a top secret e-mail that will be deleted completely from your system within one minute of its arrival. We request your company at Spy Force Headquarters on April 20 of this year. Further details will be forwarded to you once we have received your acceptance.

Regards,
R. R. Steinberger
Administration Manager
Spy Force

Clever, thought Max. She was impressed but was going to let Linden know she was onto his games. She hit *reply* to his new phony e-mail address.

From: Max Remy
To: rrsteinberger@spyforce.com
Subject: Too funny

Very funny! You must be exhausted now from being so witty.

Fond regards,
Not Easily Amused

She waited to hear back from Linden.

From: R. R. Steinberger
To: maxremy@email.com
Subject: Meeting

Dear Max,

Confused about your previous e-mail. Are you able to attend the meeting?

Regards,

R. R. Steinberger

Administration Manager

Spy Force

Max frowned as she read the e-mail again. Maybe it wasn't from Linden. He knew not to stretch a joke too far with her. But could it really be from Spy Force?

She wrote an e-mail to him using his usual address just to be sure.

From: Max Remy

To: lindenfranklin@loonmail.com

Subject: Mr. Funnyman

You might be clever. Security clearance? Meetings at Spy Force? I thought the administration manager of a major intelligence agency would be based somewhere a little classier than Mindawarra.

Max waited a few moments until a reply came back.

From: Linden Franklin

To: maxremy@email.com

Subject: What Funnyman?

Max,

I think maybe you've been sitting too close to your computer and it's starting to fry your brain. What's up with a Spy Force meeting?

Max sat back and tried to think of a witty reply, but before she had a chance, another e-mail came through.

From: Linden Franklin

To: maxremy@email.com

Subject: Spy Force e-mail

I got one too! It just arrived. A secure file. Is it really about a Spy Force meeting? What do you think they want to talk to us about? Do you think they want to send us on a mission? What are we going to tell them? How are we going to get there? This is going to be the wildest thing ever!

Max read Linden's reply three times, and each time her eyes got wider and wider as the truth sank in. The first e-mail *was* from Spy Force! What did they want? Max and Linden hadn't heard from them since the end of last summer, when they had received a telegram thanking them for their help in uncovering Blue's crooked scheme. Maybe they wanted help with a secret mission. Maybe the world was in great danger and only they, Linden and Max, could save it. Whatever it was, Max was ready. And no matter what it took, she'd get to that meeting on April 20.

Her heart beat against her chest like it suddenly didn't have enough room to keep beating. She thought about what to say in her reply. About how she was poised on the brink of possibly the most important meeting she'd ever have in her life. About how she'd probably offended a member of Spy Force. About how if only she could keep her big mouth shut . . .

"Ha ha ha."

The laughter from downstairs cackled around her room like a squawking crow had been let loose near Max's head. It was full of coy, girlish giggling and macho try-hard bellowing that sank into Max's shoulders like quick-drying glue, cementing them into what felt like hardened armor. She looked toward the door, wishing the laugh back downstairs and out of her life. She didn't care how much her mother was trying to impress fashion boy, she wasn't fooled one bit by his smarmy ways. He was as interesting as dry grass on a hot day and if her mother couldn't see it, then she was in desperate need of a major spring cleaning of her senses.

Max put on her headphones and wrote back to Spy Force.

From: Max Remy

To: rrsteinberger@spyforce.com

Subject: Meeting

Dear Mr. Steinberger,

Sorry about my previous e-mail. I thought you were someone else. Linden and I would be happy to accept your invitation to Spy Force. We await further instructions and details.

From Max Remy

She then e-mailed Linden and said she'd accepted the invitation for both of them and would get in touch when she heard more.

And this time she knew how to sign off.

From Max Remy, Superspy

CHAPTER 3

Fire Drills and a Mad Stranger

Sometimes life has an annoying way of trying to be as difficult as possible, and Max was just about to land in the middle of one of those times. Hoping for a quiet, painless day at school with as little to do with the other students as possible, she arrived the next day as the fire siren was screeching around the schoolyard like a sick rooster gone mad.

Brrurrp! Brrurrp! Brrurrp!

"Great. A fire drill," she mumbled to herself as she walked through the school gate. She saw two teachers race out of the teachers' lounge with bright yellow fire hats that kept falling down over their eyes. One of them was looking through the fire manual trying to figure out which exit she was supposed to direct the students through to escape the imaginary fire that was engulfing their school. If it was up to Max, she'd let the whole place go up in a huge technicolor bonfire that all the fire manuals in the world wouldn't be able to stop.

"Just what we need," she said under her breath. "To be herded around like cattle while the fire wardens, who just five minutes ago were ordinary teachers, direct us to who knows where as the sun beats down making sure we get a good dose of UV rays and my life flashes before my eyes in one giant wasted blur."

"Talking to yourself, Max? You know that's one of the first signs of madness. Any day now you'll start seeing your very own imaginary friend."

Toby Jennings. Of course. When days started badly, you could pretty much guarantee he'd be there to make sure it got even worse. Max was never in the mood for Toby and today was no different.

"I'm sorry," she said, determined not to let him get away with being a jerk. "You must have mistaken me for someone who actually cares about what you have to say."

"Now, Max. I'm just worried about your welfare," said Toby in his best fake-sympathetic voice. "That's why I've organized this little outing, so you and I can share some quality time together."

So Toby had set off the fire alarm. She should have guessed it was him. Being in school was bad enough, but at least in class she could be distracted from the world of losers she was surrounded by with her books and computers. Why couldn't Toby find someone else whose life he could make miserable?

"My welfare would be a whole lot better if I didn't have to share this planet with you." Max flicked her head back and walked toward the fire warden who was directing students across the street. Why, she wondered, did her life at Hollingdale seem like some terrible and mysterious punishment for a crime she never committed?

Despite doing her best to get rid of him, Toby followed closely behind Max, eager to get in another jab of his brain-dead wit. But he didn't have to. As Max reached the fire safety area, she tripped up the curb and fell face forward onto the grass in front of the entire school. She covered her head as the contents of her bag flew into the air before raining down on top of her. Now this alone would have been embarrassing enough, but Max had fallen near a leaking hose that had turned the surrounding grass into a kind of lumpy, green and brown milkshake. Max lay in the oozing mess with her eyes closed, knowing no matter how she looked, it wasn't going to be pretty.

As the first peels of laughter drowned out the fire siren, she opened her eyes and things instantly got worse. Worse than she ever could have imagined.

Toby had found her Spy Force book and was getting ready to read it out loud.

"Well, well, well. What have we got here?" he announced to the audience of laughing faces that were gathering around him.

Max wiped mud from her face and said in as threatening a voice as she could, "Give me that book now."

"Now, Max," Toby said in a sarcastic voice that made her want to scream. "You and I both know that's not going to happen. Remember? I'm the bad guy and you're the one who I have to pick on. That's the beauty of our relationship—it's so simple."

Max could feel the anger inside her heating up like a stick of dynamite about to go off. She imagined herself on the end of a giant plunger, loading Toby head-first into a cannon that would send him all the way to the other side of the world in one soaring blast.

"Now, where were we?" he asked the kids standing near him who were happy to be entertained during something that was usually really boring. "I know, I was just about to read something from Max's secret spy book."

Max cringed as she lay in the mud. A wall of legs and feet gathered closely around so that none of the teachers could see her, penning her in and making it impossible for her to get up.

Toby began to read like he was a narrator at a very bad and overacted school play.

Chronicles of Spy Force:

The rope dug into Max's and Linden's wrists as they were tied to the suspension bridge high above the vat of slimy, green jelly. The evil Mr. Blue's laughter rang out around the chrome-gray room as he told them of their fate. A slow, sticky doom awaited them, and if they didn't give him the secret code to the Time and Space Machine, they would find themselves on the night's menu as dessert. Would this be the end of Max Remy, Superspy? Would Spy Force, the secret spy organization she worked for, be able to save her? Would she be able to thwart the sinister plans of the evil Mr. Blue? Would the world be forever doomed to live without her?

"Oh no!" Toby stopped reading from the book and looked around him, getting more melodramatic by the second. "This is terrible! What are we going to do? The world won't survive without Max Remy . . ." and the next part he said like he was enjoying every syllable, "Su-per-spy."

Never before in her life had Max so badly wanted to disappear. She wished now she had her uncle's Matter Transporter control panel, so she could zap herself as far away as possible from the crush of faces leaning in and laughing.

"I hope lying in the mud wasn't your secret weapon for outwitting the evil Mr. Blue?" asked Toby like nothing was ever going to shut him up. "Because I can give you a hint: It's not going to work."

He relished the laughter that swirled around them like a whirlpool and made him feel as though he was leader of the world. He got ready to read another piece. Max watched him turn the pages and knew she had to get the book from him fast. She lunged forward from where she lay and grabbed the book at the top and bottom. Toby held on to the sides and pulled it back toward him. Max wasn't going to let go until she had her book back and was surprised at how strong her anger made her feel.

"Give it back!" Her teeth were clenched as she pulled the book toward her.

"No! Not until I've read a bit more of your amazing

spy adventures," he wheezed as he tugged the book against his chest.

That was when Max found herself doing something she'd never done before. She hadn't even had time to think about it before she realized she was surrounded by excited faces screaming, "Go! Go! Go! Go!"

Mr. Fayoud pushed his way through the students and pulled Max off Toby.

"And just what is it you think you're doing?" he shouted. His face was twisted into a purplish mix of anger and shock.

Max looked at Mr. Fayoud's oversized face leaning into her and knew she had no explanation. She rubbed together her hands, which seconds before had been around Toby's neck. This time she was in for it. She was never going to be able to explain what she'd done. She could hardly explain it to herself.

Toby ran his hands over the deep red marks on his neck.

"I don't know what I did, sir," he said, putting on his best innocent act. "One minute I was standing here obeying the fire drill, the next she tried to strangle me."

Max's mouth fell open. She looked at Toby and then down at her book. The cover had been torn off in the fight and was lying in the mud.

"You two can both go to Ms. Peasley's office. I'm sure she'll have a few things to say to the pair of you about bullying and disrupting the fire drill. As for the rest of you, the fire drill is over. Form two lines and follow your fire warden back to your classes."

There was a general moan of disappointment as everyone realized that this was probably as exciting as the day was going to get. Mr. Fayoud walked behind Max and Toby as they made their way to Ms. Peasley's office. That was never a great experience, mostly due to the floral wall hangings she painted herself out of a monthly magazine and proudly displayed. Ugh! The place was full of them and other puke-inducing stuff like embroidered signs that said A SCHOOL THAT LEARNS TOGETHER LOVES TOGETHER, and cushions on an old sofa that were shaped like love hearts. The entire place should have been shut down as a health risk for having so much phony love it could choke someone.

Either way, being marched to the principal's office was never a good thing, no matter how much stuff it had in it. Max held her breath and prepared herself for the worst.

CHAPTER 4

Two-headed Princesses and a World Full of Strife

Chronicles of Spy Force:

Alex Crane took a deep breath as she faced one of the most fearsome monsters of her life. It writhed before her like a hungry ogre, ready to feast on anything in its sight. Only this was no ordinary, foul-smelling ogre, but the two-headed, perfumed princess of the fabled land of Taraxakum, which, like Atlantis, was believed to be completely mythical. That is, until Spy Force uncovered a time slip that had for centuries kept Taraxakum hidden from the world and that the fragrant princess was using to steal precious energy reserves to power her overly aromatic land.

Taraxakum had once been a prosperous land, but when the princess ascended to the throne after her father had been eaten by a freakishly big fly, she declared that all the land's energy be employed in the making of perfumes that would be sprayed across the land in a constant sprinkle of delicate rain. Even the simplest of Taraxakumanians could see that the princess was missing a couple of floors in the brain department, but since she was the ruler, her orders were to be obeyed. This soon resulted in the running down of the economy and an extraordinary oversupply of sweet-smelling stuff. She also decreed other ludicrous laws. Flowers were to be strewn at ten-minute intervals throughout the capital and she had three Taraxakumanians with her at all times to throw rose petals at her feet so she walked across an unending bed of colorful scents. Slogans were to be written across the sky, reminding people to love each other. Schmaltzy, hideous, idiotic, mind-numbing, trashy . . .

"Max, are you listening to me?"

Max had been doing her best to avoid listening to Ms. Peasley for the last twenty minutes by thinking about another Alex Crane adventure. Why couldn't she just disappear into Alex's world forever? She was sure she wouldn't be missed and life would be a lot more pleasant than it was right now.

And it was about to get much worse.

"Yes, Ms. Peasley." She frowned, trying to look like she'd heard every word.

Being in Ms. Peasley's office was as painful as Max expected. Toby stood next to her in front of the flower-filled desk, rubbing his neck and acting as if he were in pain. There was a small trickle of blood from a scratch on his brow, but apart from that, Max was sure Toby had never felt better in his life. Especially now that she was in such trouble.

She couldn't tell what was more annoying—Toby's lame attempt at acting or Ms. Peasley's speech about how "The world is a place full of strife and turmoil and how it was up to each and every one of us to do our part to fill it with love." She said lots of other pukey stuff too that sounded like it came straight out of one of those corny self-help books displayed at supermarket checkouts. Books like, *How to Make the World a Better Place in 10 Easy Steps*. Max tried not to listen to most of it for fear that her brain would seize up in protest and never want to work again.

After the positive-guide-to-life lecture was over, Max was sent to sit in the corridor and did her best to block out Ms. Peasley's sugar-sweet voice that was still ringing in her ears like a lovesick mosquito. She was picking a piece of dried mud from her hair when, through the congealed strands, she saw her mother marching down the corridor toward her to pick her up. And to see Ms. Peasley so they could have "a word about Max's behavior."

The way her mother's footsteps echoed off the walls, it wouldn't have taken a genius to see that she wasn't happy. From the other end of the corridor she looked quite small, but each footstep made sure that soon she'd be towering over Max like a crazed giant with a sore head.

Max looked above her at the Gold Clock of Peace (it was actually called that) hanging from the ceiling by gold tinsel and realized that class was just about over. This was going to be embarrassing. Not only because the whole school was going to witness Max's mother in one of her tirades but because that same mother was being followed by Aidan! Now everyone was going to know that her mom was going out with someone who was young enough to be her son!

Why does everything in my life have to be so hard? thought Max, and almost in answer to her question, the school chime echoed around them like an invisible, cloudlike cotton ball bouncing against the walls.

"Great," Max whispered into her muddy uniform.

As the corridor filled with the multitude of arms, legs, and eyes that poured out of every class like a volcano, the once-small image of her mother now loomed over her like a huge storm cloud about to burst.

Which it soon did.

"Have you anything to say for yourself for having me dragged away from a very important lunch so that I can spend my time listening to how you've been misbehaving?"

The excited titters of the other kids flew around Max like sparks from fireworks. This was going to be even better than they expected.

Max's mother stared at her with eyes so wide they looked like two bugs under a magnifying glass. Aidan finally caught up to Max's mother and stood like a stuffed dummy behind her. Max sank as low as she could onto the bench, wishing she could disappear into the polished wood, since her mother's lecturing was only just getting started.

"And why, every time I come to pick you up from school, do you seem to be covered from head to toe with slime or mud or some other repulsive goo?"

What was Max supposed to say to that? She'd had a

few "accidents" with slimy substances in the past. Nothing out of the ordinary though, and besides, even if she had only been trying to defend herself, her mother wouldn't listen. She wouldn't have wanted to know about how Max had fallen into the mud or how Toby had stolen her book and humiliated her by reading her secret story to the whole school. She could have been kidnapped by a pack of sumo wrestlers in front of a hundred witnesses and it still would have been Max's fault. No excuse was ever good enough for having dragged her mother away from work.

Max looked at her mother's new exclusive salon haircut and expensive designer suit as she stood there waiting for an answer. What she wanted to say was, "Stop yelling at me in front of everyone. Don't you know how embarrassing it is? And what is *he* doing here? Only family members are supposed to come and pick kids up from school. You spend more time with him than me and, if it wasn't for Ms. Peasley calling you to school, you wouldn't have spent more than ten minutes with me all week."

But what she ended up saying was, "I don't know."

From the look on her mother's face, Max knew this wasn't the right answer and that she was in even more trouble than she was before.

"If you think for one minute that is any kind of reasonable explanation for your behavior, young lady, then we'll see how the next week without television alters that opinion of yours. Now wait here while I see what Ms. Peasley has to say about you."

Max wanted to warn her to sneak away before old Peasers had a chance to spout her hippie love babble all over her, but just then the door opened and Max's mother's already over-big eyes nearly rocketed out of her head when she saw a sore-looking and very bandaged Toby come out with Ms. Peasley. Toby was gently sent on his way with Peasers cooing all over him before Max's mom and Aidan were invited inside.

Phew, thought Max, relieved to have a break from her mother's flip-out, but before the principal's door closed, her mother leaned down and whispered, "Make that two weeks without television!"

Toby was instantly surrounded by kids wanting to see his bandage and hear what Peasers had said. Others were role-playing the google-eyed frenzy of Max's mom and doubling over with laughter at how funny they were.The sounds swirled around Max as if she'd been dumped in a cement mixer on maximum speed.

After what felt like an hour, Max's mother came out. She took a tissue from her purse, dabbed her cheeks, and with barely a look toward Max said, "Come with me."

The words sounded innocent enough, but as Max peeled herself off the bench, she knew they meant big trouble.

The corridor that day seemed longer than it ever had

been as Max followed her enraged mother and a quiet Aidan outside. She thought about her punishment and the fact that she'd only have to bear it for a few days since spring vacation was coming up. This meant she was only days away from escaping the smirking faces of the kids she was passing, escaping her mud-splattered life, and, most of all, escaping her mother.

Soon she'd be away from these creeps and have her friend Linden back. Max had been invited back to Aunt Eleanor and Uncle Ben's farm—where she had spent last vacation—and she couldn't get there quickly enough.

CHAPTER 5

Bad Behavior and a Vacation Nightmare

As Max and her mother drove away from Hollingdale, Max thought about what had happened in the last few hours. She'd been humiliated in front of the whole school, was covered in brown, smelly muck, and her Spy Force notebook was ruined as it lay at the bottom of her bag in two torn, mud-smudged pieces. *Her life was so miserable that at least things couldn't get any worse*, Max thought. But when they got home, things got much worse.

Her mother was in one of her "I'm-not-going-to-talk-to-you-until-you-learn-to-behave" moods. Which would have suited Max fine if she had been able to stick to it. These moods only ever lasted a few minutes, regardless of how determined her mother was to keep quiet. Her need to talk was like an out-of-control train and no matter how much anyone tried, she could never be stopped.

"Max, you and I need to have a serious talk."

Serious talk? Max knew trying to strangle Toby wasn't the smartest thing she'd ever done, but even prison would have been better than one of her mother's serious talks.

"I am very concerned about your behavior lately and just for your information, so is Ms. Peasley."

Her mother paused to give Max time to say something. Max pushed a clump of muddied hair behind her ear and had nothing to say that she thought would help, so her mother continued.

"We've decided that a few things need to change and that perhaps your complete lack of regard for other people, including that sweet boy you got into a tangle with, is perhaps connected to the lack of time you and I spend together."

Sweet boy! Toby was a lot of things but anyone who thought he was a sweet boy was having serious problems with reality!

"So we thought you and I could change that by making plans to be together."

What! Max thought. She'd just had one of the most traumatic days of her life and all that Peasley and her mother could come up with was a recipe for making it worse. She could just hear them now. Peasers blathering on about how all the world's problems could be solved with a "pinch of love" and a "dash of kindness"—Nos. 43 and 45 in *Peasers's Guide to a Better World*—and her mom going on about how mothers and daughters really are best friends; they just sometimes forget that— she would have dug that up from some women's magazine. And both of them finally agreeing to a whole lot of sickly, honey-coated stuff that would have been better off on the closest compost heap.

Max sighed as she waited to hear how this mother-and-daughter bonding time was going to be played out.

"So, instead of spending Easter on the farm, you and I are going to take a trip together," Max's mother said proudly, like it was the best idea she had ever had.

"Pardon?" Max whispered in horror.

"You and I are going to Bermuda!" she announced. "We'll book a hotel, go to the beach, eat at fancy restaurants. Spend some real time getting to know each other again. Won't it be great?"

Peasers's talk had done more damage than Max had expected. Her heart sank as she saw her time with Linden, Ben, and Eleanor fading and her hopes of being in London for her Spy Force meeting disappearing in a cloud of New Age drivel.

Max would have rather endured a ban on television, a stern talking-to, a thousand lines saying why she would never try to strangle Toby again—no matter how much he deserved it—but not a vacation with her mother!

"That sounds great," she mumbled unenthusiastically.

"I thought you'd like the idea." Her mother beamed unnaturally, as if some alien had taken over her face and was pushing up the edges into a smile.

Then there was this pause, during which neither of them knew what to say, until Max said, "I think I might go to bed."

"Okay, sweetie." Her mother sounded relieved that the awkward silence was broken.

Max made her way to her room, leaving a scattered trail of grass and dried mud behind her. Her shoulders drooped like two heavy weights had been tied to them. She turned on the computer and had two messages. One from Linden telling her how excited he was about her visit and one from Spy Force confirming their meeting on April 20. Steinberger said he would send more details in time and even added what an honor it would be to meet them. An honor!

This only made Max feel worse. She tried to write a reply to Linden, but didn't know what to say. How was she going to tell him she couldn't go to London with him? She had to think of a way out of this vacation with her mother. If she turned down this opportunity to visit Spy Force, they may never want to meet her again. All her hopes of being a superspy would be smashed forever. She turned off her computer, picked up her pajamas, and made her way to the bathroom knowing only two things: First, she needed to wash away the mud that had glued itself to her and, second, by tomorrow morning she needed a plan to save her from a trip that would be a nightmare for sure.

CHAPTER 6

Spit-firing Monsters and Last-Minute Rescue

Chronicles of Spy Force:

Alex Crane stood against the long, metal beam, bound by titanium rope, as the ragged jaws of chained crocodiles leaped toward her, missing her by inches.

But it wasn't the crocodiles that worried her most.

It was the spit-firing, giant echidna that posed her greatest threat. The pink-haired, evil overlord, Sugarlips, had lured Alex to her dungeon hideout during a mission to save the world from another of her harebrained plans. This time Sugarlips had, Pied Piper–like, enticed the children of some of the world's richest people into her lair by means of a giant mountain of cotton candy that floated sweetly above the bedrooms of the children as they slept. Their dreams became filled with images of sweet mounds of sugared heaven that drew them, sleepwalking, toward the overlord's hideout. What the children didn't know was that once they were in her sugared palace, she would place them at the mercy of the spiny-backed echidna, until their parents paid the hefty ransom she demanded of them.

Or else . . .

"Ms. Crane, time is almost up. If those parents don't deliver that ransom soon, I'm afraid some pretty nasty things will happen," Sugarlips said with a voice like melting ice cream on a hot day. "And this lovely bell here will tell us when that time comes."

Alex flinched at the sounds of Sugarlips's sickly words as she pointed to a large brass bell.

"It's no use struggling, either," she advised. "I assure you the titanium rope that binds you is as strong as any substance the world knows and you're wasting your time if you think you can get free. Besides," and at this her voice became syrupy and thick, "if you could free yourself, you would be making my precious baby very happy."

At this, the echidna sent a soaring spitball through the air. When it landed against the opposite wall of the dungeon, it spawned a fiery explosion and once the smoke cleared, a gaping, terrible hole could be seen. If the spitfire had hit a human, there was little guessing how much of that person would be left.

Alex was trapped. Caught in a world where she didn't belong with one of the most sweetly vile people she had ever met, one of the most evil of pets, and a bell set to ring out the terrible fate of innocent children. Her choice was to stay and be mauled by hungry crocs or resist and become the main course for a freakish, oversized pincushion.

Would she manage to escape and save herself from certain doom? Would she be able to free the children who had been tricked into entering this grotesque world? How was she going to stop the bell from tolling certain doom?

Brinnnggggggggggg.

"Aahhhh!"

Max shot up in bed as if the mattress had been spring-loaded. One minute she was dreaming about a terrible overlord and her pet, the next she was . . . she was . . . it took her a few seconds to realize where she was. Then everything became clear. The phone was ringing downstairs. She was in her bedroom. It was the morning of another school day. Then she remembered the worst part. She was still the girl who was doomed to spend her vacation with her mother.

Max sat there while the phone rang and watched her life fall into a tragic heap. There was nothing good about it. Nothing to look forward to. Everything was against her.

But then something happened.

"Max?"

It was her mother knocking at the door.

"Yeah?" answered Max, turning and falling into her pillow face first, hoping this would make the world go away.

It didn't, so her mother kept talking.

"Max?" She was now at close range sitting on her bed. "I've had a call from work."

She paused like she was getting ready to say something difficult. "There's a new show we are launching much earlier than expected and they want me to do it."

Max closed her eyes even tighter waiting for what calamity it would mean for her. *The world had better be careful*, she thought. *There's only so much bad news an eleven-year-old can handle.*

"Now, I know this is going to be disappointing for you, sweetie, but I'm afraid we are going to have to postpone our trip to Bermuda."

Max opened her eyes. Did she hear right? Not going to Bermuda? She was so happy she wanted to jump out of bed and swing from the light fixture.

Her mother watched as Max continued to lay face down in her pillow.

"I'm so sorry, darling. I know it was going to be so wonderful with just the two of us, but I will book another trip as soon as I can. I promise. For now though, it will mean spending your vacation at the farm."

Max thought for a minute. She sat up next to her mother, ready to lay it on as thick as she could.

"That's okay, Mom. You couldn't help it. There'll be lots of other times you and I can spend together later."

Max's mother was impressed.

"You really are the sweetest kid a parent could ever hope for. Now, how about I make you some breakfast and we get you off to school."

She kissed Max on the forehead and sprang out of the room.

It worked! Yesterday Max was the pebble in the shoe of her mother's life, condemned to weeks of punishment, today she was "the sweetest kid a parent could ever hope for." She leaped out of bed and got ready for school as if it were the best day of her life.

Spring vacation was only four days away. Max woke every morning and struck the days off her calendar as if they were layers of wrapping paper hiding a present. Nothing could upset her. Even Toby's teasing about her mother's performance at school didn't bother her. All she could think of was seeing Linden again and going to Ben and Eleanor's farm.

Finally the day arrived. The last day of school before the break. Max was waiting at the school gate for her mother to pick her up. Toby tried one parting shot before he left.

"Waiting for your mother, Max? After trying to strangle innocent children, I'm surprised she hasn't packed you off to reform school with all the other social misfits."

Max wasn't biting and besides, she could see her mother's car driving toward her and with only seconds of Toby left in her life, she didn't even bother coming up with anything nasty to say to him.

"Bye, Toby. Have a great vacation," she said brightly as she opened the car door.

Now this did two things for Max: First, it totally freaked Toby out and, second, it looked good in front of her mother that she was being nice to the boy she had been trying to strangle only days before.

Max got in the car and kissed her mother hello. As they drove off, she watched Toby, his mouth gaping wide open in shock, get smaller and smaller in the rearview mirror. She thought, *Today is a good day*.

CHAPTER 7

Ralph Attack and a Dismantled Disaster

As they drove through the rickety front gate that was hanging by a hair (Ben and Eleanor were brilliant scientists, but they knew nothing about being handy around a farm), Max could see them all there: Ben, Eleanor, Francis, and Linden. Her heart slammed in one enormous leap against her chest. She'd missed them so much since vacation, but it wasn't until she saw them again that she knew how much. The last few days blew away in a trail of dust behind her and Aidan, Peasers, Hollingdale, and Toby went with it.

When they pulled up, the following few minutes were pretty awkward and went something like this.

After the usual routine of Eleanor asking Max's mother to stay, her mother's eyes darted all over the place while she offered a few lame excuses about why she couldn't. Ben stood by, not saying much, as a few more awkward pauses made their way into the conversation before Max's mother interrupted them all by saying good-bye. She bent down and gave Max a lipsticky kiss on the cheek.

"Call me if you need anything." She winced and flicked a fly from her face. Max's mother wasn't comfortable in the country. Not one bit. "I love you, sweetie." She stepped into the car and pulled the door shut quickly after her. She wound up the window (so none of the farmland could creep in and dirty the polished leather seats), and Max watched as her mother breathed a sigh of relief and headed back to the city.

They all watched the car disappear down the dirt drive and Max wondered why her mother always had to make a quick exit when it came to her own family. She didn't even say hello to Linden or Francis.

"Let me look at you," said Eleanor, turning toward Max with a smile plastered all over her face.

She leaned down and put her hands around Max's cheeks, the folds of her dress sweeping around them like sails and they were both on the high seas. "You're even more beautiful than I remember from the last time."

No one had ever said that to Max before and she'd never thought of herself as beautiful. Ben saw that Eleanor's words made her feel uncomfortable and stepped in to save her.

"Now, Eleanor, Max doesn't need you embarrassing her in the first few minutes she's here." He put his arm around her and swooped her into the air.

"Yeah," said Linden. "There's plenty of time for Max to embarrass herself later."

Linden! It was so good to hear his jokes again. Only Max would never let him know it.

"Good to see you haven't done anything to improve your sense of humor. Wouldn't want you to change just because I'm back."

Linden smiled, glad to see Max could still be funny when she wanted to be.

There was one person left. Ben's brother, Francis. When Max and Linden had first met him in London a few months before, he was scrawny and bent-looking, with hardly enough fat on his bones to count as anything. Now he looked fit and healthy, with his cheeks full of color, his chest filled out, and it seemed he stood a whole ruler length taller.

"Hi, Francis." Max suddenly felt very shy.

"Hi," he said quietly, looking down and not knowing what to do with any of his lanky body.

A silence sat between them like a giant clump of cow manure, until something happened to get rid of it. A great leaping sack of fur burst from the verandah, jumped down the steps, and crash-landed on Max.

"Aahhh!" she yelled as her body flew through the air like a splattered pancake. This was followed by a lot of muffled cries as a mini–dust storm rose around the confusion of fur and what were once Max's upright limbs.

Ralph!

It took a few moments for everyone to realize that the affectionate mutt had escaped from his lead and was so excited by Max's return he'd forgotten all the rules of how to say a proper hello.

"Gerr 'im orff meee!" they thought they heard Max cry.

Ben and Linden charged toward the dusty muddle and pulled Ralph away, but not before he'd done a good job of covering her clothes in a solid coat of dirt and fur and her face in enough dog slobber to fill a bucket.

"I forgot about you," she growled, as she wiped her sleeve across her mouth.

Ralph whined, suspecting perhaps he'd overdone his welcome.

"Sorry about that, Max," said Eleanor. "We tied him up, but ever since he heard you were coming, he's been falling over his own tail with excitement."

It wasn't that Max didn't like animals, she just liked it better when they kept away from her. Ralph, unfortunately, never got the hint, no matter how hard she tried to let him know it.

"Linden, would you mind taking him out the back?" Eleanor asked. "You can tie him to the peach tree. Make sure he has plenty of water. We'll go inside and welcome Max in a more pleasant way."

Linden led the downhearted Ralph away as Max followed Eleanor, Francis, and Ben inside. Before she closed the door, Max stopped and looked around the farm. When she had first arrived here last vacation, she was determined to hate it, but now that she was back, it filled her with a warm, soft feeling in her stomach. It was good to be back.

But as she turned to walk through the door, a squawking cackle of feathers exploded in front of her face like a feather pillow put through a shredder.

Max pulled her head back and only just avoided the soaring, screeching attack. *The chicken!* she thought angrily, realizing that she'd only just avoided having her eyes plucked out.

"You think you're clever, don't you? Waiting until

everyone has left before you make your move," she said to the clucking lunatic who was acting all pure and sweet and pecking seed from the ground as if it hadn't done anything.

"Don't think I'm not onto you," Max warned.

The bird cackled quietly like it was smugly mumbling to itself.

"Next time you pull a stunt like that there's going to be fried chicken all around."

The chicken pecked and clucked louder, which made Max even more angry.

"And don't think I don't know what you're saying either," she hissed.

"I didn't say anything."

Max cringed as she turned around and saw Linden standing by the verandah.

"I wasn't talking to you." She frowned, annoyed that she'd been caught talking to a chicken.

"Well, who were you talking to?" he asked, acting as innocent as the chicken.

"No one."

"You were talking to Geraldine, weren't you?"

Max laughed. "As if I'd be talking to a chicken." She tried to look convincing, but even Geraldine stopped pecking and stared straight at her.

"You were talking to someone," he persisted.

Why didn't Linden ever know when it was time to let something go?

"Are you two coming inside?" asked Eleanor, popping her head out the front door.

Saved! Max thought. "Yep. Just having a look at the farm."

"A pretty close look," said Linden, as he picked a chicken feather from her hair.

"Let's go inside," Max said quickly, wanting to change the subject and suddenly remembering the other animal that had smudged itself all over her. "I need to de-Ralph myself."

Max headed straight for the bathroom, and after a complete scrubdown she went to the kitchen to find a "Welcome Back, Max" feast. Eleanor, Ben, Francis, and Linden, all wearing party hats, stood around a table so packed with food there was hardly any room for plates. There were streamers and balloons, and candles on a chocolate-covered cream-and-strawberry-filled cake, and above it a bright red banner strung across the length of the kitchen that read WE MISSED YOU, MAX.

It was another of those times in Max's life when she was looking at one of the best things ever done for her and the only thing she could think to say was, "Thanks."

As if that were the signal to start, everyone sat down and dug in. Plates were passed over heads, gravy was poured over sausages, corned beef, and vegetables, spoons clanged against bowls as mashed potatoes were scooped out and piled high next to beans, peas, beetroot, broccoli, pumpkin, yellow squash, and honeyed carrots, making everything look like giant tubes of paint had been squirted everywhere.

Eating was so quiet in Max's home. There was the correct number of matching knives and forks, small portions of food carefully arranged on plates and her mother always had on what she called her "dinner" music. Something classical or something filled with tiny bells and the sound of dolphins or whales. She'd read that it helped digestion, which Max could have told her wasn't true because it always made her want to throw up.

At the farm, dinner was filled with clanging and laughing and excited talk that flew around the table. Max was burning to know the most important thing: What state was Francis and Ben's amazing invention in?

"Is the Time and Space Machine nearly finished?"

There was a brief silence as Francis and Ben looked at each other.

"We've been a bit busy lately and haven't been able to spend as much time on it as we'd have liked," said Ben, shoveling another spoonful of peas and mashed potatoes into his mouth.

Everyone kept eating, but Max had to know more.

"So it's only a little more ahead than when I was here last?"

The Time and Space Machine had been invented by Ben and Francis and was capable of transporting matter across great distances. It had even transported Max and Linden, despite Ben's warnings that it was too dangerous. When they'd returned home (and Ben had stopped being angry with them), the two brothers began to work on it further, and it was their progress she was eager to find out about.

"In some ways, yes," stuttered Ben, shooting a quick look across at Francis.

More clanging and silence and eating. This was getting frustrating.

"In which ways?" Max was feeling a little nervous about how quiet everyone was being.

"Well, you see, Max . . ."

Max was instantly wary. When sentences started with "Well, you see, Max . . ." people were usually trying to avoid telling her something she wasn't going to like.

". . . there's been a slight hitch," Ben continued.

"What kind of hitch?" she asked slowly.

"When Francis got back to America, it wasn't long before people found out he was here and were eager to get him working again," explained Ben. "We'd started work on the machine but had to stop because Francis kept getting called away for other projects."

"So how far did you get?" asked Max, not sure if she wanted to hear the answer.

"Maybe it's best if we just show you." Ben wiped his mouth and pushed back his chair.

When they got to the shed and Max stood in front of the machine, a few things happened. First, she felt numb and tried to focus on what she was seeing, then she felt confused, which was followed by a swift feeling of anger and finally panic.

And all of this in about one minute flat.

"What happened?" she asked when her mouth started working again, after recovering from the shock.

"In order to get the machine right, we decided that we had to start from scratch. Especially since we had the Time and Space Retractor Meter that Francis brought back from London." Ben was speaking calmly, as if it were no big deal and he wasn't ruining every chance Max had of getting to London for her Spy Force meeting. "And this is how far we got."

In front of Max, and spread from one end of the shed to the other, was the Time and Space Machine, but in so many pieces, she wondered if they would ever go together again.

This was the machine that Max knew could transport matter. It was proven. Now it sat like a huge asteroid belt of boulders and space junk, with bits of the machine strewn everywhere.

Linden was just as shocked.

"I knew they'd had a setback, but I didn't know it was this far back."

Ben looked at their disappointed faces and tried to cheer them up.

"In a few months things'll calm down and the world will know about the Time and Space Machine. Just not yet."

Max and Linden sagged like two paper dolls left in the rain. All the color and shape washed away.

Ben tried again to lift their spirits. "We have made one discovery that is very important. Francis is great at desserts and has made an enormous sticky date pudding he needs help demolishing. So who wants to help us out?"

Max and Linden heard none of Ben's talking. All they could see were their hopes of going to London spelled out in the chaos of the Time and Space Machine ruins. Max had never felt so sad in her life and, barring a total reality flip or being transferred into someone else's life, she didn't know how she'd ever be happy again.

CHAPTER 8

Vomit-inducing Love Songs, Alien Eyes, and an Important Message

Max and Linden sat at Eleanor's computer and wondered what to write. They'd been staring at the screen for ten minutes and nothing had come to them.

"Maybe start with a joke," Linden suggested. "Make them feel relaxed."

Max took her eyes away from the screen briefly just to show Linden how unwelcome his suggestion was. "They're a major secret spy agency," she said. "I don't think feeling relaxed is a priority."

She turned back to the screen as she thought of the Time and Space Machine spread out across Ben's laboratory floor like a scarecrow with all its stuffing pulled out. In its small and compact form, it was capable of transporting them to London in fifteen seconds; as it was now, it wasn't capable of transporting them across the room. Her body slumped over the keyboard.

"We just have to tell them the truth," she said sadly as she started to write.

From: Max Remy

To: rrsteinberger@spyforce.com

Subject: Spy Force meeting

Dear Mr. Steinberger,

Please accept our sincerest apologies for not being able to attend the meeting at Spy Force on April 20. Due to unforeseen circumstances (like our uncle dismantling our mode of transport), we are unable to come to London at this time.

Regards,
Max and Linden

"What do you think?" she asked.

"I'm not sure. You don't think it sounds a little too casual?" he asked sarcastically.

"I want to show them we aren't kids."

"But we are kids," said Linden, not understanding why Max found it so hard to be herself sometimes.

"You know what I mean." She snapped and pressed *send*—and the message was gone.

They both sat staring at the empty screen.

"What do you think they wanted to meet us for?" asked Linden.

"I guess we'll never know." As Max said this, she felt even sadder.

Outside, Ralph whined as if he were just as disappointed as they were.

"Coming, fella." Linden leaned toward the window and waved. "Better go. It's my turn to have Ralph and he doesn't like getting home after dark."

Linden stood up from the desk.

"Don't worry, Max. My mom used to say when one door closes, another opens. You'll see. Something will happen next that will be great."

He waited for Max to say something but she didn't.

"See you tomorrow, then," he said and left the room.

Linden's words floated around Max's head like flying ants she wished would go away. When doors closed in Max's life, other ones locked ever tighter. When her dad went away, her mom became bossy and never seemed as relaxed as she used to be. When she left her last school and best friend, she ended up at Hollingdale, where no one liked her. She wanted to believe Linden, but she knew her life too well to know things worked any differently.

She shut down the computer and went to the kitchen to say good night, but stopped when she was met with the three backsides of Ben, Eleanor, and Francis, whose heads were poking out the kitchen window into the yard.

"What's going on?"

"It's Larry," said Eleanor. "He's been building a haystack out here for an hour."

Larry was a pig who predicted the weather. Or at least that's what Max had been told. She wasn't convinced this wasn't just Ben, Eleanor, and Linden nursing a mild dose of lunacy.

"What does that mean?" asked Max, curious despite her skepticism.

"Means there's going to be a windstorm," said Ben, without a shred of doubt in his voice. "A big one, judging by the size of that stack."

Max stared at all three rear ends as they continued to poke their heads out the window.

"Why a haystack?" asked Max, not sure why she even asked.

"He likes to see them tumble down when the wind comes up," said Ben, chuckling. "Gets a real kick out of it."

That was all Max needed to know about Larry and his haystack for now. She suddenly felt tired and didn't want to talk any more.

"'Night, then." She turned to leave them to their staring.

"Would you like me to come and tuck you in?" asked Eleanor, bringing her head in from outside.

"No, I'll be all right," said Max and dragged herself to bed.

When she woke up the next morning, Max didn't open her eyes right away. The sound of Ben and Eleanor singing a soppy love song filtered into her room like the smell of rotting fish in the sun. Max loved Ben and Eleanor, but if they could sing in tune it wouldn't have been quite as terrible. To add to that, the morning was hot and steamy with a warm breeze blowing directly onto her face, which nearly made her pass out with the smell of the farm it carried with it.

"Country life stinks sometimes," she mumbled, referring to the smell and her memory of the broken Time and Space Machine. But when she opened her eyes, she was met with something even more terrible. Two bulging, bloodshot eyes she was sure belonged to a weird, psychopathic alien.

Her heart pounded as she faced the fierce creature and remembered something.

She remembered to scream.

"Aahhh!"

The alien eyes became bigger and even more bloodshot before disappearing under the bed as Ben and Eleanor rushed into the room.

"What is it?" they asked, pushing their faces into hers.

"It was . . . I saw . . . I think . . ." said Max, not knowing what it was.

"Take your time, Max. Tell us what happened," said Eleanor gently, just as a whimper was heard from beneath the bed.

Max's eyes narrowed. "Ralph," she whispered, as she saw images of the ragged mutt being packed off to the other side of the world on a very, *very* slow boat.

Ben plunged under the bed as Eleanor winced. "Sorry, Max. We told him to stay outside. Normally he's very obedient, but he's taken such a liking to you he doesn't seem to listen to a word we say."

"Come on, Ralph. That's your fun for the day over," Ben wheezed as he pulled the reluctant canine out. "It's the doghouse for you, sunshine."

Ralph looked over his shoulder at a scowling Max as he crept outside after Ben.

"Why doesn't he get that I don't like him?"

"He can't help it. It's that magnetic personality of yours." Linden was standing at the door munching on a pepper.

Sometimes Linden did that. It was as if he never walked into a room but would somehow just appear.

"How about some breakfast and you can try out more of your eagerly awaited humor then?" said Eleanor, looking at Max and smiling.

Linden opened his mouth to say something else, but, before he could, the phone rang. "Maybe I'll just get that."

"You'd be doing the world a great favor," said Max. "Or at least this part of it."

Eleanor sat down on the bed next to Max.

"I'm sorry about Ralph. He's usually so shy. Looks like you've brought out the wild side in him."

"Great. I won't be chalking that up as one of my talents."

"Max!" Linden called from the hall. "Phone for you."

Max froze. Maybe it was Spy Force calling with a plan to get them to London. Or maybe they were going to bring the meeting here. Or maybe it was . . .

"It's your mom."

My *mom!* she thought, as she got out of bed and walked to the phone. *What does she want?*

Linden put his hand over the receiver and almost in answer to her thought said, "She wants to know how you're doing."

"How I'm doing?" Max asked incredulously. Her mother

never called to see how she was doing. "She must have cooked up some other way to ruin my life."

Linden handed her the receiver.

"Hello," she said, warily.

Pause.

"Yep, I'm fine," she said, not sounding fine at all.

Another pause. Longer this time.

"Sounds great." But the way Max said it, whatever her mother said didn't seem great at all.

An even longer pause and then, "Okay, 'bye."

Max hung up and stared at the phone. "Peasers! That speech of hers really worked its way into Mom's head and I'm the one who's going to have to pay for it."

"What did she say?" asked Linden.

"She wants to spend a lot more time with me when I get back. Wants to sit with me while I do my homework. Make quality time every afternoon to talk about our days and share our feelings."

"Are you sure it was your mother?" asked Linden.

"Sounded like her. And she wants us to share time with Aidan."

Linden had heard all about Aidan from Max's e-mail; he was her mom's new boyfriend, and Linden knew Max wasn't thrilled about him.

"So the forecast is bad?"

"Couldn't be worse." Max turned and made her way to the kitchen.

But after breakfast, something happened to change everything. Max and Linden were sitting at Eleanor's computer when an e-mail from R.R. Steinberger arrived. It had one simple message:

> Don't worry about transport problems. All will be taken care of. Be in the back paddock at eight o'clock tonight.

And that was it.

"What does it mean?" asked Linden.

"Not sure, but I guess we'd better be in the paddock at eight o'clock to find out," Max said slowly, letting the message sink in. "And that we're going to be at that Spy Force meeting after all."

Max and Linden stared at the screen before turning and smiling at each other.

"Aaaahhhh!" they both screamed excitedly.

Eleanor rushed in to see what was wrong.

"What happened?" she asked, worried that it was another animal attack.

Max and Linden looked at each other. They couldn't let Eleanor know what they were planning. She'd think it was too dangerous and try to stop them. Max had wanted to be a spy all her life and she couldn't risk anything spoiling it now.

"Nothing," she said, trying to think of a cover. "Linden just told another one of his jokes." She smiled, pleased that she could make a dig at his humor.

"Maybe you could hold off on being funny for the rest of the day, Linden. I think my heart has had about as much as it can take of it for one morning." Eleanor gave a half-smile, half-frown as she left the room.

Max was pleased with her quick thinking. "Sorry. Just had to get that in."

"It's okay. It's your way of coping with being in the presence of great comedy."

"So that's what they're calling it these days, are they?" she asked.

"You better believe it." Linden smiled. Max did have a sense of humor when she wanted to.

"What about your dad?" asked Max. "Won't he wonder where you are?"

"He's away for a few days at a farming conference," said Linden. "I was supposed to stay at Ben and Eleanor's the whole time anyway."

They both turned to the screen. After all Max had been through in the last few days, it felt as if the world were finally going her way. She'd have given anything to go to London. Even spending more time with fashion-tragic Aidan didn't seem so bad now.

A smile trickled onto her lips as she knew her life was about to change forever.

[illegible]

[illegible]

[illegible]

[illegible]

[illegible]

[illegible]

[illegible]

[illegible]

[illegible]

CHAPTER 9

A Giant Windstorm and a Mysterious Landing

Chronicles of Spy Force:

Alex Crane looked out from her precarious position balanced on the tip of the mast of the sailing ship *Inferno* and knew that now that help had arrived, her life, which was teetering on the edge of oblivion, would be saved.

"Max! Thank heavens you're here," she called through the panicked squall of wind and rain that lashed against them.

Max was new to the business, but even with little solid experience, she was proving to be one of the best spies Alex Crane had ever come across.

Brilliant. Clever. A natural.

"We've only got minutes before this whole ship is blown into the sky and us with it," Alex said into her lapel transceiver in her usual direct and unflappable manner.

Max knew she had to think, and fast. The wind buffeted against her like an overzealous bully as she dangled by a rope from the battered helicopter overhead. The aircraft swayed above them like a cancan dancer, its blades kicking out against the blue-black sky, lit by the angry flare of lightning.

She operated the helicopter by remote control, trying to maneuver herself closer to the mast and Alex before the lit fuse inside the vessel ignited the cargo of deadly explosives.

All she had to do was expertly guide the helicopter closer, making sure a sudden updraft didn't spin it out of control and send it spiraling into the sea. Just a little closer toward Alex and she would . . .

"Max?"

The voice behind her made her jump, sending her pen sliding across the page and her backside bouncing off the log she was perched on so she landed unglamorously on the ground. Legs splayed, head hurting, and her fingers softly nestled in a warm cushion of chicken poop.

"Sorry," Eleanor apologized. "I didn't mean to scare you."

"That's okay." Max glared at Geraldine who clucked loudly and pranced away as if she'd just laid a golden egg.

"I didn't hear you coming." Max pulled herself back onto the log and looked for something to wipe her hand on. She never understood why she ended up on the ground more times than the average eleven-year-old did.

"I just wanted to tell you that we're so happy to have you back."

Max looked through her book to find a blank page to clean her fingers with. Also to avoid further embarrassment because she could feel herself blushing at what Eleanor had said.

"The place didn't feel the same when you left."

Max looked up. Eleanor had this smile that made Max feel all warm inside.

"How's school?" Eleanor asked.

"Good," said Max. She'd been concentrating so much on Alex Crane that she'd totally forgotten about everything at home. The farm had a way of doing that.

"And your mom?" Eleanor was twisting a ring on her finger. Max's mom had one exactly like it that she kept in a silver box. Max knew that because she'd take it out and wear it when her mother wasn't home. It had a red stone and was set in a gold bed of interlinked roses.

"She's good."

"That's good." But the way Eleanor looked away when she said this made Max think something wasn't quite right.

"Where did you get the ring?"

Eleanor noticed she'd been playing with it and stopped.

"Just before your gran died, she gave identical ones to me and your mother, asking us always to look out for each other."

Eleanor sat quietly staring at the ring.

"Why don't you and Mom get along?" Max asked.

"Now there's a question." Eleanor clasped her hands and looked at the horizon. "Even when we were little girls, we weren't very close. It's just always been that way. I think that's why Gran gave us the rings. She hoped it would bring us closer together."

She drew the colorful layers of her skirt around her

knees so she looked like the inside of a kaleidoscope. Her face creased into a sad frown.

"She has a boyfriend now," Max informed her.

"Really?" Eleanor was curious to know more and Max was happy to tell her, but she wasn't going to sugarcoat anything. She was going to tell it exactly like it was.

"But he's a real jerk who spends a lot of money dressing like he hasn't got any, stays in the bathroom so long he might as well move in there, and wears so much aftershave there should be a pollution warning put out whenever he leaves the house."

"So you're not a fan?" Eleanor asked in a serious tone, making Max think she may have overdone it a little.

"Not much." She looked at her clothing and brushed off the grass and mud.

They sat in silence for a few seconds.

Max was disappointed. She was hoping Eleanor would be on her side.

"Even though he does sound like a real jerk." Eleanor smirked and tried to stop herself from laughing.

Max looked up from her fingers and smiled too. Then Eleanor started to laugh. So did Max. They laughed even harder until they were holding their stomachs and giggling so loudly that crows in the trees nearby swooped away in fright. They rocked back and forth with laughter until they toppled backward and both fell off the log straight into another fresh batch of chicken poop.

This time Max didn't care and didn't see Geraldine as she scratched in the dirt as if she were doing a victory dance. They just kept laughing and lying on the ground.

"Were you thinking about something funny I said earlier?" An upside-down Linden was staring at them from overhead.

"Yep, that's exactly what happened," Eleanor chuckled, catching her breath and sitting up before helping Max to her feet. "And now that we've got that out of our systems, I'd better go and give Ben a hand with dinner."

She laughed to herself as she walked away, the layers of her skirt creating a trail of dust behind her with each giggle.

"What was that all about?" asked Linden.

"I told Eleanor a joke and she thought it was the funniest one she'd ever heard."

"She doesn't get out much," explained Linden.

Max smiled. Linden was good.

"Let's go and eat. We've got an appointment to keep."

After dinner Max and Linden excused themselves and walked toward the paddock. It had been arranged that they'd stay at Linden's house for the night and would make their way back the next day, which gave them lots of time for their meeting. Except that when Ben and Eleanor said good-bye, there was something about the way they said it that felt a little more important than usual. Like they knew something. Max thought she was probably being paranoid and they headed off into the dusk.

"Have you done your hair?" Wild strands of Linden's hair were ballooning into the air like towers on miniature bouncing castles. "We *are* about to go to a very important meeting after all."

"I even put on some of Dad's hair gel." But the look on Max's face told him it hadn't done much good. "Mom used to say I've got hair with a lot of personality—what can I do? And besides, you can't keep a good strand down."

He giggled at his own joke. Max tried to ignore the joke and his hair and walked on.

"Where should we wait?" asked Linden.

"Not sure. I guess we should just go somewhere in the middle," Max answered, starting to feel nervous about the whole thing and hoping she didn't mess up.

They walked a little farther as Linden started to guess how they might get to London.

"Maybe they're going to send some little green men in a super-advanced spaceship to take us away?" he suggested.

Max's nerves got worse. She pictured herself walking into Spy Force's plush secret headquarters and at the earliest possible chance, falling down in front of everyone.

"Or maybe they're going to use a high-density matter scrambler to dismantle the atoms from our bodies, fling them through space at the speed of light, and reassemble them in London."

Linden was getting more excited at the possibility of what might happen. Max, on the other hand, wasn't. Her head was jammed with images of disaster, like the one where she was being introduced to the head of Spy Force and accidentally knocked hot coffee from the table all over him. Or the one where she attempted to clip on her fingerprint-sensitive identity pass and accidentally flicked it across the room, breaking the invisible laser beam that set off a high-security alert. She could see the chaos as she tried to apologize among the running feet and barked orders of Spy Force's top security agents.

Linden, oblivious of her panic, talked on.

"Or maybe we'll be sucked into space at a million miles an hour in a giant strawlike transporter tunnel and spat out at Spy Force headquarters."

Max had had enough of Linden's speculating.

"Or maybe you should just keep quiet so they don't hear how much you talk and decide not to meet us at all."

Linden stopped abruptly, as if an enormous cement wall had suddenly dropped in front of him. He thought it was fun trying to figure out what might happen.

Max walked on until she found a place that looked like all the others and decided to stop.

"I think here is a good spot," she announced, and sat down and checked through her pack to see if she had everything.

Linden followed her, wondering what it was about Max that made her so hard to understand. One minute she was fine, the next she wasn't. He sat down beside her, deciding it was best not to think too much about it.

"What's that?"

Max flinched as a muffled ringing sound was heard from somewhere close by.

"I brought the CTR just in case we need it," Linden explained as he rummaged through his pocket.

"Great," said Max, not sounding at all like she thought it was great.

"Hello?" Linden asked, followed by a quick and surprised, "Ella!" as if it could have been anybody else. "How are you?"

The CTR was a Communication Tracking and Recording device that Ella had given Linden on their last mission in London. Max knew it could come in handy, but refused to like anything about Ella so she wasn't about to admit it. She sat slightly away from him as he blahed on and on with a lot of *really's* and *no way's* and *that's great's*.

After a few minutes Max couldn't stand it anymore. She snatched the device from Linden's hand, spied a large rock nearby and threw the CTR so hard it made fireworks in the sky in a million pieces. She watched as it all happened in slow motion. First the throw, then the flying curve through the air, and finally the impact, sending sparks and CTR bits everywhere in an impressive, airlifted shower.

"Thanks for calling. I'll speak to you later."

Max never snatched away the CTR and Linden finished his conversation oblivious of her imagined outburst.

"That was Ella."

Max didn't respond but looked toward the darkening horizon.

"She said Blue has this new range of kid's foods that she and her mom are convinced can't be good."

Max tried not to listen but couldn't help perking up at the mention of Blue's name. "They think that if Blue is behind it there has to be something bad about it. Trouble is, the stuff tastes so good that once you've had some you can't get enough. You know, like those hamburger chains that sell you burgers that make you feel queasy afterward but you keep going back and buying more."

Max was dying to ask about Blue's foods but refused to act interested.

"Maybe that's why Spy Force wants to see us," Linden persisted.

"Maybe." Max shrugged, thinking he was probably right.

"Oh, and she said to say hi."

Max looked down at her watch and really pretended not to hear this one.

"It's almost eight o'clock. I guess we just wait now."

Linden sighed and put the CTR safely back in his pocket. He didn't understand why Max didn't like

Ella, but knew she'd have to come around one day.

They sat in silence for ages. Nothing much happened, apart from a few owl hootings and the odd rustling of grass nearby, which Max told herself was the innocent scrambling of lizards and not the sneaky slithering of deadly brown snakes.

There were certain things in the country Max still couldn't get used to.

"What was that?" She jumped up in a panic as something fluttered quickly past her face.

"Moth most likely," said Linden calmly, watching her hands swish frantically around her like a human fan on high speed.

"They can get as big as small birds out here. Can't hurt you, though. Any sign?"

Max stopped waving her hands, put them on her hips and looked around, trying to pretend she wasn't spooked.

"Not yet." She sat down and started to feel calmer. Linden had a way of doing that. When she felt nervous, he would say things that made her feel okay again. Max relaxed for the first time in ages. "Little green men?" she asked.

"Okay, so it's more likely we'll be collected in the transporter tunnel," Linden said authoritatively.

They both smiled and sat there again, waiting for what would happen next.

"We should say our pact," Linden suggested.

Max cringed. She was hoping to get through this part of

their mission without having to go through any soppy stuff. "I think it's better we stay quiet in case we miss anything."

"You know I'm not going until we do it. I think it's important."

Why did Linden do this? thought Max. Mostly he was pretty easygoing, but there were times he had this look on his face that told her he was going to get what he wanted.

"Okay." She sighed. "How does it go again?"

Linden held out his hands and closed his eyes.

"Oh, that's right," Max wilted. "The holding hands bit. My favorite part."

"If Max should come to harm or get lost or be in danger in any way, I, Linden M. Franklin, will do everything I can to help her and bring her to safety."

Max squinted through half-closed eyes for something that would interrupt this overly sentimental moment. Nothing happened so she tried to remember the pact.

"If Linden should get into trouble . . ."

". . . come to harm," he corrected.

". . . come to harm," Max struggled to remember. "Or get lost or be in danger in any way, I, Max Remy, will um, will um, help him out . . ."

". . . do everything I can . . ."

". . . do everything I can to help him and bring him to safety."

"Now that wasn't too hard, was it?" Linden smiled and let go of Max's hands.

Pleased now that it was over, Max looked at her watch again for what felt like the hundredth time.

"It's almost nine o'clock," she said frowning. "Maybe they've forgotten about us."

"I don't think that's possible. You're a pretty hard person to forget."

"Is that right?" Max replied. She was about to let fly with something witty when they felt the ground beneath them start to vibrate.

"Can you feel that?" she asked.

"Either I've developed a bad twitch or we're about to find out what the e-mail from Spy Force meant." Linden put his hands on the ground and looked around.

The vibrating became more intense, like a gigantic steamroller was coming toward them.

"What do you think it is?" Max strained her eyes to see through the dark.

"Not sure, but it's something big."

"What should we do?"

"I don't think we've got much choice but to sit here and shake."

Just as Linden finished saying this, a mighty thump shook the ground. They closed their eyes as a powerful gust of wind swept around them, encircling them in dust and almost lifting them into the air.

"Aaahhh!" Max and Linden held onto each.

After a few minutes the vibrations decreased and the

wind dropped down like someone had switched off a huge propeller.

And then, nothing.

Max and Linden looked around them. Their hair was plastered upward, and their teeth were gleaming white against their dirt-covered skin. Apart from that, everything seemed like it was before until they realized one horrible thing.

They had their arms around each other.

"Errrrrrr!" they screamed and pulled away, quickly wiping their hands against their clothes to brush away the hug as much as the dirt that had caked itself to them.

"What happened?" Linden wiped his eyes so that he left two dirtless stripes like he was wearing a bank robber's mask.

"I can't see anything." Then Max remembered. "Maybe it was that windstorm Larry predicted."

"He's got a good nose for weather that pig." Linden smiled proudly.

Max was getting annoyed. "Where are they? They said they'd be here," she said huffily. "We've been waiting over an hour and—"

Before she could say any more, a mechanical hum began to whir in front of them from the inky night blackness. Max and Linden squinted hard to see what it was and couldn't keep their mouths from falling open when they saw what happened next. A large metal hatch was being slowly lowered to the ground. Nothing else. Just a large metal hatch.

"Maybe it's the alien theory after all." Linden gasped, not sure he was ready to have his first extra-terrestrial encounter.

A silhouetted figure stepped forward as if between two walls of light that poured out of the hatch in a blinding flood.

Max and Linden sat wide-eyed and frozen like two rabbits caught in headlights as the mysterious figure loomed before them.

"I guess it's too late to make a run for it?" joked Linden, hoping to ease the tension.

It didn't. Before Max could answer, the figure removed a long, solid object from its pocket, stepped down the hatch and headed straight toward them. They nervously imagined what the object could be. A gun. A knife. A Spectral Atom Pulverizer (this was Linden's thought, not Max's).

Whatever it was, Max and Linden watched the figure getting closer and closer, knowing they could be facing the final, terrible moments of their lives.

CHAPTER 10

A Wild Ride

"Max?"

"Yeah."

"If you survive and I don't, could you make sure my goldfish Henry gets fed?"

"You'll survive," said Max, trying to figure out what their next move should be.

"And could you let my dad know he's the best?"

"Linden, nothing is going to happen to you," she shot back, his questions pestering her like a small yapping dog.

The figure got closer. The long object in his hand dangled like a slow pendulum with each step, as if it were counting down the last minutes of their lives.

"I've also got a subscription to *Spy Monthly* that will need to be cancelled. And I have—"

Max had had enough. "Linden. If you keep going, the only person you'll have to be worried about is me."

He got the point and was quiet.

The silhouette stopped a few yards in front of them. The light from the hatch formed an angelic halo all around him. Max and Linden huddled together, desperately thinking what to do. Then slowly, menacingly, the figure raised the long, slender object so that it was pointing straight at them.

"What are we going to do?" Max whispered as her brief life flashed before her eyes like a video clip on fast forward.

Then something happened to answer her. The figure

moved the object even closer toward them and muttered one, short word.

"Mint?"

Both of them frowned.

"Did you say 'mint'?" asked Linden, double-checking that he'd heard right.

"Yep. They're the chewy kind. My favorite," said the figure.

There seemed nothing much else to do but accept.

"Thanks," said Linden, relieved to be alive as the figure dropped mints into their hands.

"No matter how many times I do it, I can never quite get used to the effect this whole travel thing has on me. Leaves me sort of light-headed. Takes me a good few minutes to get my mouth working again. I guess it has something to do with the speed. Not quite as fast as light yet, but they're working on that. Even though some scientists think it's impossible, what with the infinite amount of energy needed to push an object through space at that speed. But I guess people thought we'd never walk on the moon until Armstrong put on a spacesuit one day and up and did it."

The strange man who was getting stranger by the second, paused long enough to realize he hadn't told them his name.

"Oh! How rude of me. I haven't introduced myself. I'm Steinberger. R.R. Steinberger. Administration Manager of

Spy Force. And you are Max Remy and Linden Franklin. Pleased to meet you both."

He held out his hand.

It was hard to believe that the person who had sent Max such brief and formal e-mails could turn out to be this man with a mouth like a running tap.

Max and Linden held out their hands but before they could make contact, they heard a beeping sound.

"Oh." Steinberger took out what looked like a mini-computer from his pocket, disappointed to have to end the conversation so quickly. "Looks like the jet's ready for takeoff."

This was too much.

"The jet? What jet?" Max wondered if perhaps this Steinberger person had lost a few rungs on the ladder when it came to the brain department.

"Oh, I haven't mentioned that yet?" He laughed. "Silly me. The superfast, deluxe TXR-5 Invisible Jet that's behind us."

He flung his arms out like he was a game show host introducing the grand prize.

"An invisible jet?" asked Linden, looking at nothing but a well-lit hatch.

"Yep. Only one of its kind. Except for the TXJ-7, but we don't like to mention that one because it tends to get Frond upset over the issue of fuel consumption. A little guzzler it was, but we soon fixed that so that now this one runs on a purely plant-based formula that creates no pollution whatsoever. In fact—"

Beep, beep, beep, beep!

Steinberger was again interrupted by the pager.

"It's Sleek. He tends to get upset if we don't keep on schedule, and after that unfortunate incident with the weather balloon on the way here, we're already a bit behind. Shall we?" He moved toward the hatch.

Max and Linden stood up and cautiously followed him, wondering if taking this strange man's lead was a very wise thing to do, while a million questions crash-landed in their heads. Who was Frond? What was a "Sleek"? How is it possible to have an invisible jet? And why did this guy talk so much?

As they approached the hatch, Steinberger stood aside and invited them in.

"Welcome to your superfast ride to London in the world's most luxurious, high-tech mode of transport to ever—"

"Steinberger!" called an agitated voice.

"Right you are, Sleek," he replied, and ushered them quickly in.

The entrance to the hatch was blocked by two glowing balloonlike walls. Max and Linden looked at each other and shrugged before pushing their way in. Once inside, they found themselves in a small, white, rubber room. They could hear ticking.

"What's going on?" But just as Linden asked this, an alarm bell sounded and a blast of vacuumlike air lifted them off their feet. It sucked at their hair and clothes, whisking them around in circles and bouncing them off the soft walls.

"Aaahhh!" they screamed.

Max felt dizzy and hoped she wasn't getting her brain sucked out.

They were bounced and twirled and jostled in a fierce vacuum frenzy. Then suddenly the suction stopped and they were spat out of the balloon chamber and left tumbling around, trying to regain their balance.

Max was starting to get annoyed at how they were being treated but before she let Steinberger have it, she took a good look around at where they'd landed.

They really were inside a jet! And it was enormous. There were fluffy, lined seats and carpets, digital screens that folded out from the armrests, giant beanbags, a glass cabinet filled with every drink imaginable, a spa, and even a small pool.

Steinberger stepped out of the chamber and patted down his ruffled hair. He looked very apologetic.

"I'm sorry about that. I should have warned you about our Automatic People Sanitizer. When a passenger steps into the jet, the sanitizer detects if there is any material on them that may interfere with the smooth running of the machine—dirt and dust, for example—and it turns itself on if it thinks a good clean is needed. Very efficient for getting rid of any pesky bugs or cleaning up after a particularly messy mission, and I can tell you there have been plenty of—"

"This is your captain speaking," interrupted a stern message on the intercom. "Would all cabin crew and passengers get ready for takeoff. Make sure your tray tables are stowed correctly and your seat belts are firmly fastened. Takeoff will be in approximately thirty seconds."

Max and Linden were shown to their fluffy seats by a tall, unsmiling, uniformed man who asked if they were comfortable and without waiting for a reply, went to the back of the jet and strapped himself into a seat.

"We're a little pressed for time," Steinberger said, explaining the apparent rudeness as he took a seat opposite them.

The jet silently rose a few yards into the air, rotated so that it faced the opposite direction, and took off into the night at a powerful speed. Max and Linden were pressed into their seats by the force of the takeoff and could only just manage to look out the windows as the jet flew high above the ground.

"Well, here we are," Steinberger announced, smoothing down his notepad that had been mangled in the sanitizer. "If there are any questions you'd like to ask about the plane or Spy Force, fire away. I'm here to be your personal guide. In fact, you might even want to know a little about me. I'd be flattered to help you out there, it's a fascinating—"

"What is this?" Linden interrupted, fearing another long-winded jabberfest, and pressed a large silver button beside him. Before Steinberger could answer, digital screens rose out of Linden's armrest and turned to face him.

"Those are some of technology's finest," Steinberger declared proudly. "They are Digital Think Amajigs with Triple Megapixel Microdrive and integrated audio with Hyper Blaster Sound compatibility. You can do all sorts of things with these, including ordering food, which you might like to do now. Just tell the computer what you'd like and Roger, our friendly cabin assistant, will bring it to you."

Max activated hers, and she and Linden typed in their requests on the touch screens. Chocolate ice cream with caramel sauce and sprinkles for Linden and a banana smoothie with yogurt and honey for Max.

"Your request will be here momentarily," announced the computers.

"I knew there was something missing in my home." Linden pictured himself with a brand new computer in his room. Then he remembered there was something else he wanted to know as well. "How can you make a jet invisible?"

"Ah, terrific question," beamed Steinberger, leaning forward and almost falling off his seat. "A few years ago Irene was in the middle of one of her experiments, mixing all sorts of concoctions together, when she added a special liquid that was to be the finishing touch and all of a sudden what she was working on just disappeared. At first she thought it was her eyes playing tricks on her—she's not as young as she used to be, as she'll probably tell you when you meet her—but when she realized she could see everything else perfectly, she knew she had hit upon something remarkable. After a few more adjustments in the lab, Spy Force perfected and patented it. All rights belong to us and, I'm sure I don't have to tell you, the formula is top secret."

Max and Linden were impressed.

"Is Irene one of your scientists?" asked Max.

"No. She works in the kitchen. Makes a mean sponge cake."

Steinberger's eyes went droopy just thinking about it.

The jet sped silently and smoothly through the night sky like a stingray gliding through the ocean.

"What can you tell us about the meeting?" asked Max, eager to know more about what they could expect.

"Ah, that is the one thing I've been asked to keep

quiet about until your arrival in London. I *can* say it's for something very important, but until we get to Spy Force, I'm afraid I can't say anymore." Steinberger turned his fingers in front of his mouth like he was locking his lips shut.

"What can you tell us about Spy Force?" Max probed further.

"There's lots to tell there." Steinberger folded his hands in front of him and sat back in his pink fluffy chair. "It was created in the early 1960s by Harrison Senior, the father of the current Chief of Spy Force, who is also called Harrison. Harrison Senior and his father, Pop Harrison Senior, were top chefs at one of the finest restaurants in London, which was called Harrison's, naturally enough. Anyway, one day, the two decided they needed a career change and putting their heads together, came up with an international agency for fighting crime everywhere, which they called Spy Force, or the Security Protection Unit For Ousting Rotten Crime Everywhere. That spells Spy Force when you work it out."

Max and Linden ran it through their heads.

"No, it doesn't. It spells Spu-force," Linden advised quietly.

Steinberger shifted uneasily in his chair.

"Well, the, err, Marketing Department thought having an international spy agency called Spu-force might be bad for business. You know. Sounds like spew-force. People might joke and call it Vomit Force. So they decided just to fudge it a little."

Just then, the steward arrived with their orders. Linden's tastebuds turned over themselves as he tucked into the best, creamiest ice cream he'd ever had in his life.

"Homemade. You can't take the chef out of the chief," Steinberger mused dreamily.

"How long does the jet take to get to London?" queried Max, slowly sipping her smoothie to savor each taste-tickling mouthful.

Steinberger looked at his watch.

"Should be there . . . about . . . now," he declared.

In a flash, the steward reappeared, grabbed their plates and glasses mid-slurp, and disappeared toward the back of the jet.

"This is your captain speaking," said the voice on the intercom.

"He loves saying that," whispered Steinberger excitedly.

"We will be arriving in London shortly. Remember what I said about the tray tables and seat belts and get ready for a smooth landing."

Max and Linden tightened their belts and looked out at the city of London below. The jet's windows were a blur of old buildings, towers, palaces, churches, and cathedrals. Roads wound through like ant trails swarming with cars, trucks, motorcycles, pedestrians, and lurching black cabs, while the Thames River snaked its way under bridges that crisscrossed over it like antique matchsticks.

Max looked down at the city and took a deep gulp of air as she tried to take in what was about to happen. In just a little while, she and Linden would be face-to-face with the world's top spies.

CHAPTER 11

VARTS, Vibrations, and Spy Force!

Chronicles of Spy Force:

It was the largest gathering of secret agents the world had never known. A top-secret affair with security at its highest level. And with good reason. It wasn't every day that the world's top spies assembled together under the same roof. In fact, it was only once a year, during the annual Spy Awards Night, a prestigious event that recognized the talents, skills, and contributions of spies from all over the world. Spy Force often topped the bill for the night, taking home many of the awards, including the coveted and highly respected Spy Agency of the Year award.

The rest of the world never knew about these events. If they ever did know, the existence of these intelligence networks would be in grave jeopardy; many would even cease to exist as soon as news got out.

The location of the ceremony was announced only the day before and, even then, just the chiefs of the organizations were informed. Since technology could sometimes be tampered with, they were told by specially trained mynah birds, the perfect messengers, as they worked in pairs and always delivered. A secret rendezvous point would be arranged where the chiefs and mynah birds would meet and the message would be tweeted out in a few short cheeps before the birds would fly innocently away. Very discreet, very professional, and very top secret.

This year was a highly unusual type of awards night.

This year a new spy who had been recruited by Spy Force was causing a stir throughout the ranks of spies everywhere. She was changing the face of intelligence work with feats of daring and skill the spy world had never seen before.

This spy's name was Max Remy.

But many knew her as Max Remy, Superspy.

As clusters of intelligence agents hushed over dimly lit tables, spoke in secret whispers, and quietly applauded each award winner, most were anxiously awaiting the announcement of who would be Spy of the Year.

As the head of the Academy of World Spies approached the podium, the room fell silent. In just a few moments, she would announce the Spy of the Year. An honor bestowed on the bravest, most intelligent spy who had made the world a safer, better place.

"And the winner is," the head of the academy began as she pried open the specially sealed gold envelope, "Max Remy!"

Max's hands sprang to her mouth in shock. She was not only brave and intelligent, she was also a very humble person, not used to such attention. Alex Crane leaned over from her seat and gave Max a hug.

"You deserve this," she whispered proudly to her one-time protégé.

Max stood up, her legs becoming jellylike beneath her,

and made her way to the podium. She accepted the statue of the Golden Spy Binoculars, held it against her chest and began her speech.

"I would like to thank the Academy for this very generous and unexpected award. Ever since I was a little girl, I've wanted to be a spy and do all I can to make this world safer for people everywhere. I dedicate this award to spies all over the world who risk their lives every day for the same cause. I would like to thank Spy Force for believing in me, and Alex Crane for being my mentor, my guide, and my inspiration."

The room exploded with the emotional clapping of agents as they applauded in admiration of the spy they could only hope to be. Max looked around the room at the awestruck faces and gave a small bow. Soon there was a hushed call of "Max" from the audience. Then another. Then another. Until soon, the whole room echoed with the quiet chanting of "Max, Max, Max."

Max held her award high above her head.

The applause continued on . . .

"Max!" cried Linden.

Max snapped out of her daydream.

"Are you coming or not?" Linden was standing at the

door of the jet, wondering when Max was going to get off.

She looked around her. They'd landed. She wasn't sure where, but she quickly undid her seat belt to find out.

"Sure," she said, rushing to the hatch and feeling as if she'd overslept for an important exam.

"I'm glad to see you've finally decided to join us, Ms. Remy," Linden remarked in a teacherly voice. "This tardy attitude of yours is going to do you no favors, young lady. And another thing—"

"Linden," Max warned. "It's not too late to hand your body over for medical research, you know."

Linden's mouth collapsed open in an attempt at looking offended.

"And what would you do for entertainment then?"

"I'd watch grass grow or paint dry, something as funny as you."

"It's time to go," interrupted Steinberger, poking his head into the jet.

Max and Linden stepped out onto a boardwalk-style metal deck. They were inside a cavernous, shiny aircraft hangar. Everything was quiet except for a low motorized hum and the echoing noises made by their footsteps. Dim lights hung from the towering roof above them like stars in a miniature universe, just barely revealing a pristine, orderly metal cavern filled with all kinds of contraptions and vehicles. There were all-terrain trucks, submarines, planes, helicopters, one-seater mini-choppers, hovercrafts, gliders, and an array of other machines they'd never seen before.

A man dressed in overalls lay on his back on the floor below the metal deck.

"What's he doing?" asked Linden, wondering why the man's hands were clutching tools and working away in thin air.

"He's servicing the jet now that we've returned," Steinberger explained. "He's also the pilot. Let me introduce you."

He moved closer to the edge of the deck.

"Sleek, these are our esteemed passengers, Linden Franklin and Max Remy."

The overalled man kept working on the invisible jet and gasped a mysterious reply that sounded something like, "eeooorr ooo ahhh inmyanr."

"Sleek gets very focused when he's busy," Steinberger informed them in a hushed voice. "This is our Vehicular All-Response Tower, or VART for short, and Sleek is crucial to this part of Spy Force. Not only does he fly and know everything there is to know about all these aeronautical thingamajiggies, he's our extreme member of the team. No mountain is too high, no high-speed chase too fast, and no vat of worms too icky for him. You name anything extreme that has happened in Spy Force, and Sleek has been there."

Just then, a black cat jumped from behind them down to the ground where Sleek lay working. In a single reflex action, Sleek moved his head sideways and noticed the cat staring straight at him.

"Aaaahh!" he yelled and performed a maneuver that astounded Max and Linden so much, their eyes only just managed to stay in their sockets. He leaped from the floor, completed a double backflip, and landed on the deck, which was a whole ten feet above him, in one swift move. He stood next to Max, open-mouthed and google-eyed, as if someone had stretched his head long-ways and forgotten to put it back to normal. The black cat caught her eye and then walked away with what Max thought were arrogant and calculated steps. A steely tremor ran through her as she was caught by the cat's gaze.

Sleek, meanwhile, noticing that the others were staring at him, closed his mouth, ungoogled his eyes, and tried to pretend everything was fine.

"I think that's all for today," he said, wiping his hands on an oilcloth he pulled from his pocket. "Jet's in good condition. Enjoy your visit." And with that he walked off, trying hard to look relaxed, but all he managed to do was look terribly awkward.

"One of the bravest men I know." Steinberger looked after him admiringly. "The cat belongs to Dretch, our maintenance operator. Her name's Delilah and she's taken quite a liking to Sleek, but he's not too good with black cats or other superstitious things. Apart from that, though, he's one of our best. Now,"—he clapped his hands together—"let's go and meet everyone else."

He walked off with clipped, excited steps, mumbling to himself and consulting his handheld computer.

Max felt uneasy.

"There's something about that cat I don't like," she whispered to Linden.

Linden stopped walking. His eyebrows reached new heights of incredulity as they arched up his forehead.

"Max, you're a person with a lot of talents, but I think it's only fair to tell you, an affinity for animals isn't one of them."

"I'm fine with animals," she protested.

"Which ones?"

Max was stumped.

"That's not the point. That cat looked at me and gave me a strange feeling."

"I wouldn't take it personally. Cats are really perceptive and she just needs more time to realize that deep down you really are an animal lover."

Linden's grin spread over his face before he hurried to catch up with Steinberger. Max turned around and saw Delilah sitting in a corner licking her fur and acting no more suspicious than any other house cat. *Maybe Linden was right*, she thought, but she'd keep her eye out if Delilah crossed her path again.

Max was doing her best to take everything in, including the fact that what she thought was a fictitious spy agency was now all around her. She was at Spy Force, the international intelligence agency, bursting at its high-tech seams with spies, missions, intrigue, and top-secret secrets to save the world. Important stuff that was unlike any part of her regular life. She heard nothing of what Steinberger was saying to Linden as the three of them walked along the gleaming deck. She looked up at the VART's roof with its twinkling low-level lights and sighed, knowing her life would never be the same again. Would be filled from now on with—

Booof!

Silence. Except for the quiet motorized humming.

"Max, are you all right?"

The room blurred in front of her eyes like a thick, swirling fog.

"Can you hear us, Max? How many fingers am I holding up?"

Max could see little snippets of Linden and Steinberger through a churning, confused mist. Molecules of man and boy floated past her, urging her to understand what they meant.

Then . . .

"Urgh! What is that?"

She sat upright, holding her nose.

"A little something they came up with in the lab. Instantly revives you if you've had a temporary collapse," explained Steinberger, removing a small brown bottle from beneath her nose.

"Or, in your case, if you've run into an enormous and pretty unmissable giant metal cylinder." Linden smiled.

Max rubbed the spot on her forehead that was starting to blush into a deep, red welt. The type of welt that comes up just before a bruise and a big, ugly-looking lump.

"Maybe they should bottle your jokes instead, because they sure smell enough to bring back the dead," Max shot back.

"She's fine," diagnosed Linden. "Only a conscious Max could have a comeback like that."

"What's in that stuff?" she grizzled, wincing and breathing out hard to get the stinky potion out of her nostrils.

"All natural ingredients." Steinberger smiled, relieved that his young guest still seemed to be in one piece. "Nature can be just as smelly as chemicals when she wants to be."

Holding his minicomputer in front of him, Steinberger checked over his list.

"And now we must go. There's so little to see and so much time to do it in."

He looked up and frowned.

"Why do I feel like I've just quoted a line from a famous book?"

He rubbed his hand across his chin trying to figure it out.

Max stared at him with her throbbing head, wishing he'd get on with it.

"Oh well, not to worry. Let's continue with our expedition, shall we?"

Steinberger pivoted on his overzealous feet and cracked a quick pace along the deck and out of the VART. The sound of his clicking heels echoed around the hangar like a cicada-filled summer day, as Linden put on a quick double-step to keep up. *If the hangar for the aircraft was this big, then the rest of Spy Force must be enormous*, he thought, enjoying every minute of their tour.

Max lagged behind, annoyed at finding herself on the ground once again and especially annoyed at the lack of sympathy she'd received over her aching head.

Steinberger and Linden stopped before a darkened exit. Max eventually joined them.

"Before we go any farther, you need to step onto the Vibratron 5000 and have your vibrations recorded."

"Vibra-what?" asked Max, thinking some of Steinberger's brain cells must have come loose during their high-speed flight.

"The Vibratron 5000. There is one at every possible entry point into Spy Force. All you need to do is step onto these specially sensitized tiles that will read the vibrations of your body."

"And why would I want to do that?" blurted out Max, thinking she was going to be pushed around again, just as she had been in the Automatic People Sanitizer.

"It's one way we identify people who enter the agency," Steinberger continued, not seeming to notice Max's bad mood at all. "The floors throughout Spy Force are made out of a specially constructed material that is very absorbent, very quiet, and can identify the person walking on them merely by reading their vibrations."

"That's excellent!" Linden exclaimed. But Max was dubious as she looked down at the arrangement of dark tiles at her feet.

"Would you like to go first?" Steinberger asked her, as if he were granting her some great wish.

Thinking she'd probably regret it, Max stepped carefully onto the tiles. As soon as she did, they lit up in a rich, pulsing red color like burning hot coals. She became nervous, but when she tried to jump off, her shoes felt as if they were glued to the floor. She was about to scream when a gentle buzz trembled inside her like a million soft drink bubbles making their way up her body.

Then . . . *Ping!* The red pulsing light faded and the process was finished.

"Now anywhere you go in Spy Force you can be positively identified. Linden?"

Linden jumped on quickly as soon as Max got out of the way, ready to experience the full force of the Vibratron 5000.

The tiles lit up again and Linden's face broke into a wide smile as the bubble effect tingled throughout his body.

"Good, isn't it?" asked Steinberger, remembering his first experience on the device. "It's never quite the same after the first time. Now, on with the rest of the tour."

Steinberger turned down a corridor that seemed to go on forever. Small lights on either side of the floor and ceiling disappeared far away, so that it looked like the three of them were walking in space. He marched quickly ahead, blathering away and pointing out other special characteristics of the building.

Suddenly a small, bent man appeared in front of Max and Linden, stopping them dead in their tracks. His eyes burrowed into them from behind half-closed lids and a long gray fringe that sagged in front of his face like stringy old washing. A ragged scar ran the length of his cheek and down past his gray stubbled chin before it disappeared into the collar of his shirt. His hands were buried in a deep maroon coat that hung limply over two spindly, insect-thin legs and long white socks like chalk sticks that crept up to his buckled knees.

"What are you doing here?" he snarled at them as Delilah appeared from nowhere and jumped into his arms.

Max and Linden felt the temperature around them drop as Steinberger walked on, prattling merrily to himself, oblivious of the mysterious stranger's sudden and unexpected appearance.

Max tried to explain.

"We're—"

"I know who you are," the old man snapped, running his bony fingers along the length of the purring feline. "I know everything that goes on around here. Just don't think you're anyone important because you've been given some kind of special invitation to this place. Others like you have come before and have never been seen again. So be warned. Stay out of my way and you'll stand a chance of getting out of here in one piece . . . if you get out at all."

"Ah, Dretch," Steinberger called from down the corridor, turning to see where Max and Linden were. "I see you've met our two guests."

Steinberger clopped gaily toward them as Dretch leaned down and whispered an icy caution.

"I've got no intention of playing nursemaid to you two, so don't come looking to me for help when you get into trouble," he spat, like he'd had more than his fair share of meanness handed out to him at birth.

By this time Steinberger was standing next to them.

"Let me introduce you properly," he said. "My guess is Dretch has been too modest about himself and has neglected to tell you that he is one of the best agents Spy Force has ever known. He now works exclusively on-site as our maintenance expert at the agency and I can tell you, if it weren't for him, this place would have fallen apart a long time ago.'

Dretch looked away. Whether because it wasn't true or because he had something to hide, Max couldn't tell.

"And of course you already know Delilah. Here kitty," cooed Steinberger, but as he tried to pat her, she offered a disgruntled hiss and turned her head away. "Well, ah, we must keep moving. There are a few more things we need to do before we meet Harrison," he said, ticking something off on his notepad.

Max thought she saw Dretch flinch when he heard the name Harrison, but after what he'd said to them, she thought it also could have been because of his instant dislike of them.

Steinberger walked down the corridor. Before Max and Linden could follow him, Dretch left them with one final word of warning.

"Watch your backs, kiddies. Because if you don't, something bad might happen and it would be a terrible shame to lose our new guests so early in their visit."

He stepped aside for them to catch up to Steinberger.

Max and Linden's heads swam with a mix of fear and curiosity as they moved past the crooked old man. Who was he and why was he so mean?

And what did he mean when he said others had come before and had never been seen again? And what happened to change him from a top agent to a maintenance man?

Max and Linden stuck close to Steinberger, deciding to avoid Dretch as much as they could, but something about what he said echoed in Max's mind like a beacon warning ships of treacherous rocks ahead.

CHAPTER 12

Slimy Toadstools and a Wall of Goodness

"Go on, try it."

Max and Linden sat in the glare of the Spy Force canteen lights. Black-suited adults moved around them ordering multicolored muffins, crunching on striped toast, and sipping hot pink coffee. It was morning teatime and the canteen was busy. They sat beside Steinberger, looked at the lumpy green concoction in front of them, and tried to think of a way of getting out of having any.

"It looks really lovely," Max fibbed. "But I'm still full from the banana smoothie I had on the jet."

"Yeah," added Linden, rummaging through his brain for his own excuse. "That ice cream really filled me up, too."

Steinberger chopped into the cake like it was made with the best-tasting ingredients in the world.

"I don't know what it is, but I just can't get enough of Irene's sponge cakes. Take my word for it, you won't regret it." He pushed the bulging, baked mess on the platter closer to both of them. "Go on. Just try a bit. If that's not the best piece of cake you've ever had, you can stand me on my head and call me Charlie."

Steinberger was getting stranger and stranger by the minute, and pouring another helping of fluorescent blue, gooey stuff over the slime-green muck on his plate only proved it further. Max and Linden didn't want to offend him, especially since they might need his help if they ran into Dretch again. They reached for a spoon and squelched out two minuscule portions.

The spoon made a kind of sucking sound as it made its way out of the gloopy frog-colored mess. Maybe that's what gave it its color, mashed frogs, Linden thought as he stared at the Kermit-tinted spoon in front of him. Max looked at hers and held her breath, thinking that at least if she blocked her nose she wouldn't taste very much of it. They took one last look at each other and in a silent countdown to three, closed their eyes and prepared to sample the vile-looking paste. As soon as the spoon touched their mouths, however, something wonderful happened. It was as if their tongues were being zapped by the yummiest tastes ever.

"Wow, these spies really know their food," Linden squished through another mouthful of cake. "Even if the color scheme's a little bizarre."

"What's even more bizarre is a life that's got no color in it at all," boomed a voice behind them, velvety and smooth like a rich chocolate sauce.

"Ah, Irene," said Steinberger, wiping away two splotches of fluorescent-blue gunk lighting up the corners of his mouth. "Max, Linden, and I were just admiring your latest work of art."

"So these are our two little visitors, eh? Welcome to Spy Force and to my newest creation—the Slimy Toadstool."

So this was Irene. The inventor of the invisible jet formula. She was a rounded woman, wearing almost every color imaginable so that she looked like a human carousel. She had bright-orange hair, red glasses, rose-colored earrings, and a bright dress that raced around her curves like the blurred colors of a Formula One track. Her apron was decorated like a tropical greenhouse and her shoes were made in the shape of green tree frogs. Irene obviously wasn't asked to do any undercover work.

"Everything our Irene touches is always original and always tasty," declared Steinberger. "Why, she used to be one of London's finest chefs before coming here."

"Yeah, but I got sick of making tasty meals for skinny girls worried about being fat when they should have been more worried about being blown over in the wind," complained Irene, waving her hands all over the place and just missing a spy carrying a plate of blue sausages balanced on a pillow of red mash. "And men whose clothes cost more than a small country makes in a year with no interest in anyone's conversations but their own. Oh, the fame was good. Lots of perks and all. Even got invited to afternoon tea with the Queen once. But I'm not as young as I used to be and didn't want to waste any more time with people like that, so I joined Spy Force. Haven't looked back since. Anyway, got to get back. Harrison's got a meeting with some important people from Brazil later and needs something special whipped up."

And with that, Irene was off along the steaming dishes crammed with their unusual creations before swooping through the swinging kitchen doors like a toucan nose-diving for her next meal.

Steinberger finished off his last piece of Toadstool and wiped his mouth.

"Ah," he sighed. "That hit the spot. Now we're ready to meet the rest of the team. Come with me."

Max and Linden hurriedly scraped their plates clean of green-blue cake, not wanting to waste a morsel, but as Max stood up, her head thumped into something hard above her, sending plates, cutlery, and a wobbling, orange concoction flying through the air. Now, normally, everything would have landed all over her, covering her with some kind of muck, so she flung her hands over her head ready to be slimed. But when the crashing stopped and she realized she was fine, she opened her eyes and turned to see what damage had been done.

Crouching on the floor near her was a small man with his hands pressed against his ears. The wobbling orange concoction slithered down his hair and what was once a crisp, white labcoat.

"Everything's fine, Plomb. Just a simple accident."

Steinberger was kneeling next to the man, looking into his eyes and talking slow and weird as if he had peanut butter stuck to his teeth and he were trying to get it off.

"These are our two guests I was telling you about. Max and Linden."

The man looked around but didn't take his hands away from his ears.

"Pleased to meet you," he said in a voice so soft that Max and Linden could hardly hear him. He then gave a small smile before quickly standing, stepping over the broken pile of fallen plates, and hurrying out of the place.

"Who was that?" asked Linden.

"That was Professor Plomb, our bomb expert." Steinberger stood up and wiped some orange goop from his shoulder.

"Why did he look so scared?" asked Max, feeling bad because she'd made him run off so suddenly.

"He doesn't like loud noises."

"Isn't that a bit of a disadvantage for a bomb expert?" Linden frowned.

"It actually works out quite well," Steinberger pointed out as he made his way toward the canteen exit. "His father was a bomb expert and his father before him. Plomb had always wanted to be a world-class surfer until he realized he had an extreme case of hydrophobia, which left him with an unfortunate inability to go in the water. No good for a world-champion surfer, of course, so he said good-bye to his watery ambitions and followed in his father's footsteps making bombs. But he did it by making his own special mark. All the bombs he makes are silent."

"Silent bombs?" Max and Linden asked together.

"Yep. He's brilliant at them. Great for enabling Spy

Force to infiltrate places without being heard. He makes all kinds, too: stink bombs, tear bombs, colored fart-gas bombs. He normally doesn't come out of his foam-walled lab, but it looks like Irene has her orange and pumpkin mousse on today. He can never say no to that."

Black-suited agents slid past them in the corridor like silent shadows, speaking in quiet mutterings into small palm-sized gadgets, whispering to each other in darkened corners or quietly hurrying by as if they were on their way to an important mission.

Steinberger pulled out his minicomputer and, looking at his list, gradually came to a slow stop.

"Ah," he said with a withering look. "Frond is next."

His expression became all glazed and dreamy-eyed.

Max and Linden gave each other a quick look. Max had seen this kind of behavior before. She sighed and screwed up her face into an annoyed grimace.

"Um, Mr. Steinberger?" she said, trying to snap him out of it so they could get on with the tour.

Steinberger didn't budge and instead was now humming some kind of off-key love tune.

"Mr. Steinberger?" she said a little louder.

Still nothing.

Max pursed her lips. She'd had enough of this schmaltzy drivel.

"Quick! Fire!" she yelled as loudly as she could.

"Where? What? Who?" stammered Steinberger as he spun around and tried to figure out what the emergency was.

Agents near them stopped in their tracks. They stared at the two young strangers and rested their steady fingers against their jackets, ready to reach for the secret weapons concealed inside.

Steinberger stopped spinning and, seeing that everything was fine, realized he'd possibly been a little preoccupied.

"Sorry about that." He blushed. "All seems under control now, everyone," he said to the agents who lowered their hands and cautiously continued on their way.

Linden made a bad attempt at hiding a smile as Steinberger pushed his hair back into place and tried to look a little more normal.

"Let's get on with it, shall we?" He was doing his best to sound professional. "Otherwise we'll be late for our meeting with the boss himself."

Harrison! Max and Linden's faces were wiped clear of grimaces and smiles as they followed Steinberger down the hall and remembered their meeting. What would the head of a major spy organization be like? And what did he want with them when he had the responsibility of the whole world to look after? Whatever the answer, if he flew them halfway across the world, it must be important.

At the end of the corridor they stopped and faced what Max and Linden quickly figured out was the end of the corridor.

No doors. No windows. Nothing.

With her hands firmly placed on her hips, Max swung around to face Steinberger.

"And now?" she asked in a voice that couldn't be described as her most polite.

"Now for the best part." Steinberger was unable to contain his excitement and missed the Max attitude altogether. "This is called the Wall of Goodness. There isn't another wall like it in the entire world," he said importantly.

"The Wall of Goodness? What happens here?" Linden was drawn into Steinberger's enthusiasm and was keen to have another Vibratron 5000 experience.

"This is the entrance to the part of Spy Force that is restricted access and requires a further level of identification. As you will know, the location and layout of Spy Force is a heavily guarded secret from most of the outside world. Other areas of our agency such as the canteen, the sleeping quarters, and the Finance Department, are low-security areas, but where we are about to enter, is the inner sanctum of the force," he said grandly, like he was in the middle of an important scene from *Star Wars*.

"What about the Vibratron 5000? Isn't that enough to identify who we are?" Max was getting a little impatient and wasn't sure all this drama was necessary.

"To a certain extent, yes," Steinberger's *Star Wars* voice continued. "But the Wall of Goodness acts as an advanced form of the old-fashioned lie detector. It has been made with a super-malleable substance that has been programmed to read bodily reactions to establish a person's current state of goodness. Only if it recognizes you as a good person will it permit you entry."

"Has it ever recognized anyone as being bad?" Linden was intrigued.

Steinberger's face fell into a hurt scowl as though he were remembering something painful.

"Only once."

"Who was it?" Linden breathed, hanging on every word of the story.

"An agent who was expelled from the Force in unhappy circumstances."

"A Spy Force agent?" gasped Linden.

"Yes. He'd stolen someone's vibrations, got past the Vibratron, and was headed for the nerve center of the Force when the Wall of Goodness raised the alarm and one of the most dangerous infiltrations of Spy Force was narrowly averted."

Linden was stupefied. This was better than any spy story he'd ever read.

A few seconds of silence passed as Max stared at the two starstruck goons she was standing with.

"I really hate to break up this dramatic moment but do you think we could get on with it before I reach my next birthday?"

"You're right." Steinberger collected himself and looked at his watch. "Time is running a bit short. This next step we can all do together to save time. Just stare directly at the Wall of Goodness and stand as still as you can. You will notice it start to move like jelly. That's the wall's atoms reconfiguring at the approach of a human being and going into identification mode. It will then reach out and envelop you. Nothing more spectacular than *Terminator* I'm afraid, but it's still pretty good when you see it up close. After a few moments it will take a reading of your vital signs and your level of goodness before totally surrounding you and absorbing you into the heart of Spy Force."

Great, thought Max. *Why does everything in this place have to be so complicated?*

Max, Linden, and Steinberger stared at the wall in front of them. After a few seconds, everything happened just as they were told, except that when the wall oozed out and wrapped itself around them, it felt like warm, sticky custard. It squelched all over them and, within a few seconds, Steinberger was sucked into the squishy structure in one quick slurp.

Linden's eyes widened as if they'd suddenly doubled in size.

"Wow! Did you see that?" he gasped, finding it hard to speak while the wall kneaded him like a ball of human dough.

"Despite the fact that I'm being mauled by a half-crazed wall, I can still see, you know," Max retorted.

And then, just as the words were out of her mouth, Linden also disappeared in a guzzling splurt.

As the gooey body search continued, Max was definitely running out of the tiny scrap of patience she had left.

"Look, Wall. Let me save you the trouble. I'm good, okay? So can I just go in now?"

The Wall of Goodness seemed to be having trouble deciding whether to let Max pass. It made choking, gurgling noises and jostled her around even more, so that the massage became more like the spin cycle of a washing machine.

Max started to worry that she wasn't going to get through.

"Come . . . on . . . Wall. Pl . . . ease?" she wobbled.

After one final heaving lurch, the wall totally enveloped her and she was gone, reforming its atoms and leaving nothing more than a solid stone structure that looked impenetrable.

CHAPTER 13
SLOPPP!

"Whaaa!" exclaimed Max as she was thrust headfirst out the other side of the Wall of Goodness into a gaping tangle of lush fern leaves.

"Congratulations!" Steinberger exclaimed to her awkwardly positioned backside sticking out of the fern. "You made it. It's one of the toughest tests within Spy Force. You don't have to be truly evil to be denied entry. The wall will even stop people simply for not having the best interests of the agency at heart. Anyway, how was it?"

Max weeded herself out of the clinging fronds to see Linden's and Steinberger's eyes lit up like fireworks on New Year's Eve.

Only she hadn't been invited to the party.

She was furious.

"How was it?" The way she asked the question, Linden knew her answer wasn't going to be pretty. "I was just mauled by an arrogant wall that slobbered all over me like elephant's drool and treated me as though I was a leftover piece of modeling clay. And when it'd finally had enough of me, it sputtered me out face first into this pile of nature clutter."

Steinberger was disappointed that Max didn't seem to have enjoyed her experience.

"You did unfortunately have a rather bumpy landing," he apologized. "Most people come out of it a little more gently than you did. In fact, that's the first time I've seen anyone have such a rough landing."

Max plucked greenery from her hair and dropped it to the floor.

"Max has many talents, Mr. Steinberger, but gentle landings isn't one of them." Linden's explanation failed to amuse Max and earned him one of her well-measured glares.

"Thanks, Mr. Hilarious. The world has just become a better place now that it can add that joke to its list."

"I assure you both that is the last of our identification procedures," Steinberger promised. "If you'd like to make your way through the green aisle in front of us, we will meet our next important Spy Force agent."

They were in a multilevel greenhouse where there seemed to be almost every kind of plant in the world. There were weeping willows, oaks, eucalyptus, jacarandas, fruit trees, flowers of all kinds, multicolored algae, mosses and funguses splattered on rocks and cliffs, cactuses in special desert areas, palms, shrubs, bulbs, grasses, vines, and water lilies.

Max strode ahead at Steinberger's invitation, careful not to trip over any vines or roots that might be lying in front of her.

"Don't worry about her." Linden leaned into Steinberger. "She really is a nice person. It just doesn't come as naturally to her as it does to other people."

Linden smiled a sweeping grin before he and Steinberger made their way down the palm-strewn pathway.

Among all the greenery were white-coated people beavering away like termites building a vast natural city. They were spraying, weeding, pruning, clipping, and watering. They were leaning over boiling pots, crushing roots, extracting oils, and dissecting delicate flower stems. Some were even standing on small white platforms hovering like dragonflies at the tops of the tallest trees.

In the middle of the greenhouse was a woman in a long red coat with her hair piled up on her head like an overloaded beehive. Small flying bugs could be seen zooming in and out of the swaying mass of hair as if they'd made their home there. She had little round glasses shaped like roses and a chain hanging from them that looked like red and yellow ladybugs.

When Max and Linden reached the woman, Steinberger was nowhere in sight.

"You must be our two guests." She smiled widely. "My name is Dr. Frond. I'm in charge of the Plantorium here at Spy Force. Have you come here alone?"

Almost in answer to her question, a splash was heard somewhere behind them.

"Steinberger's here, isn't he?" asked Frond. "Quick, grab that rope will you?"

Linden reached behind him and took a rope that was hanging beneath Frond's workbench. Both he and Max followed her as she wove effortlessly through an intricate maze of plants, her red coat swishing behind her like a red light on a rescue truck.

"The Japanese pond. I thought so," said Frond as they stood in front of a rich turquoise pool teaming with giant goldfish. She took the rope from Linden and threw it to a waterlogged Steinberger.

"Ah . . . Frond," he managed soggily, once he'd been hauled out of the water. "How lovely to, ah, see you. Um, nice day outside."

He had a lily pad perched on his head, a string of reeds dangling from his left ear, and a flustered and peeved-looking goldfish poking out of his top pocket.

Max and Linden wondered when it was that the normally calm and collected Steinberger had been replaced with the bungling, stammering idiot standing in front of them.

"I think you'll find it's been raining," Frond replied to Steinberger's misguided weather report. She gently rescued the fish from his pocket and returned it to the pond. It gave what Max thought was a scowl before it flipped around and swam away.

Then something happened that twisted the puzzled expressions on Max's and Linden's faces even further.

Steinberger was at a loss for words.

He had nothing to say.

They could see the normally free-flowing words getting stuck somewhere between his throat and his blushing red face, which screwed up as if he'd been given some horrible stew he was being forced to eat and was threatening to go down the wrong way.

Linden thought he'd save the situation from becoming even more awkward than it already was.

"What happens in the Plantorium?"

There was an almost audible sigh of relief from everyone, especially Max, who thought if she had to deal with any more of Steinberger's gooey-eyed mush, her brain would come screaming out of her head in protest.

"This is where we make the serums, potions, powders, creams, lotions, pills, and ointments that are used in Spy Force operations. We use only natural and plant-based ingredients to make our products, and, of course, we never test them on animals. We here at Spy Force believe that animals are human too and plants can do as much as chemicals when it comes to fighting crime. And let's face it, we're not in the twentieth century anymore. If you don't have a green-beating heart, you're behind the times."

"What kinds of products do you make?" queried Max, thinking the Plantorium sounded more like a cosmetic factory than the important arm of a major spy agency.

"Come and I'll show you. Do we have time, Steinberger?"

Silence.

Max and Linden turned around to see him staring at Frond like someone had sucked the insides out of his head and turned him into a zombie.

"Well?" Max's patience was really being given a good workout. "Do we have time?"

"Time?"

Glazed eyes. Lilting mouth. Steinberger had it bad.

"Time to see what Dr. Frond has to show us?"

"There's always time for Dr. Frond," he spouted, and a great slooshing smile swung onto his cheeks.

Max and Linden continued to stare at him.

Steinberger noticed their staring and looked sharply down at his watch.

"I mean, yes, there is a little time before we have to move on," he said more seriously.

"Good. Follow me." Frond swished her red coat around her and eagerly scurried through the trees.

At one corner of the Plantorium, across a thick patch of woolly butt grass (it's actually called that) and through a heavily flowered wall of mimosa bush, was a frosted glass door. Frond opened the mossy hatch on a small algae-covered panel and pressed in a secret code. The door clicked open and allowed them all inside to what looked like a giant pharmacy. There were long gleaming white shelves that ran so high it was hard to see where they ended and the ceiling began. They stretched far back into the room like rows of schoolkids during an assembly, and nestled on each one were all sizes and shapes of bottles, tubes, jars, containers, boxes, and cans.

"We call this room the Secret Library for Ointments, Powders, and Plant Products, or SLOPPP for short."

Frond stepped up to one of the shelves and took down a small glass jar.

"This is invisible cream," she announced like she was holding a precious stone. "With just a thin layer of this cream applied to the skin, a person will become completely invisible. Some scientific theory dates the origin of the cream back to the ancient Egyptians. Why, there is a group of historians who believe invisibility creams had been in use in the ancient world for hundreds of years."

Max and Linden were impressed.

"Try some," she offered, but seeing their hesitation, Frond asked Steinberger if he wouldn't mind volunteering.

He managed to take a small step forward but failed miserably in trying to get his mouth to work. He flinched slightly as she took his hand and winced when a low giggle escaped from his lips.

"This is very powerful stuff." She took a small swipe of the dark-green cream and rubbed it into Steinberger's hand. "It can even be watered down and applied as a rinse if you need to become invisible in a hurry. All you need is the smallest amount, and there you have it."

It was hard to tell if Steinberger was enjoying the experience or was about to pass out at any second, but what was easy to see, or rather not to see, was his disappearing hand.

The invisibility cream worked!

"And here . . ." gasped Frond as she stretched for a jar almost out of her reach, ". . . is the antidote. Just a little of this and all will return to normal."

Steinberger quivered as Frond's fingers dipped into the blue-black antidote and were coming straight for him. Little beads of sweat appeared on his forehead like balls of fluff on woolen socks.

"Done." She finished applying the cream and, like a wave pulling away from the beach, Steinberger's hand reappeared. "And that's just one of the many products we've developed here at the Plantorium. There are many more but I'm sure you have to be on your way. Harrison doesn't like to be kept waiting."

"Dr. Frond?" asked Max, picking up a bottle of purple liquid near her labeled "Stun Perfume No. 5." "What is the story with the labels?"

Pasted across the front of all the items on SLOPPP's shelves were green and gold labels that read "Plantorium Health Co.," and beneath that was the slogan "Your health is our business (A Kind to Trees initiative)."

"This is one of the commercial sides of the Force," explained Frond. "While experimenting with plants, we have come up with an array of natural products that have many benefits in everyday life. Wrinkle creams, anti-sag ointments, buttocks-firming lotions. That last one in particular is very popular and is one of Spy Force's biggest sellers.

As long as there are sagging bottoms and wrinkled brows, we'll be in business for a long time. It costs a lot of money to run a spy agency and in these days of budget cuts and strict cost-cutting measures, we have to do all we can to stay in business."

Max was perplexed.

"So it's not good enough just to try and find bad guys and make the world a better place?"

"In the old days. And in the movies, of course. But saving the world is an expensive business and we've got to earn our keep. This is our way of doing just that."

Beep, beep, beep, beep!

Everyone looked down at Steinberger's pocket, which seemed to be beeping. Everyone except Steinberger, of course, who was busy trying to remember how to breathe and listen to Frond at the same time.

Frond offered a crooked smile. "That'll be Harrison, I expect."

At the mention of Harrison, Steinberger's eyes snapped wide open. He reached into his pocket and pulled out his minicomputer, and, after removing from the screen some green slime he'd picked up from the pond, read the message.

"So it is. Well, must be off. It's time to find out the real reason you've been asked to Spy Force."

Steinberger stood in front of Frond and fretted over how to say good-bye. Suddenly he felt like every inch of him was on display and that any part of him could embarrass him terribly at any moment. He smiled painfully, then found he had the hiccups. He wiped sweat beads from his brow that were forming so fast they were like ants that'd found a picnic. Finally, he held out his hand, but as he did so Frond lifted hers to wave good-bye. They both laughed awkwardly. Then as Frond lowered her hand, Steinberger raised his. They laughed again and lowered both their hands, at which point Steinberger dropped his pencil. As he bent down to pick it up, so did Frond, and their heads collided in a thudding bump.

Max was hoping this was going to be over soon before someone really got hurt.

"'Bye," Steinberger muttered to Frond. Rubbing his brow, he turned sharply and collided with one of the shelves, sending Plantorium products cascading domino-style into a pile of all-natural mess.

He apologized to Frond and offered to clean up but Frond refused, saying it would be better if they were off.

Steinberger managed a muffled "Thank you" and turned to leave the SLOPPP, followed by Linden and Max.

"Good thing love doesn't make everyone this clumsy or hospitals would be filled with bleeding hearts and lovesick fracture cases," said Linden.

"Better off without it at all," complained Max, watching Steinberger trap his finger in the door and wondering how he'd got this far in life. "For now, though, we've got to worry about what Harrison wants."

Steinberger's injuries quickly faded from Max's and Linden's minds as their thoughts focused on the next few moments in front of them, which were going to put them directly in the middle of possibly the most important meeting of their lives.

Max steeled herself.

I'm ready, she thought. *Spy Force, here I come.*

CHAPTER 14

Meeting the Chief and an Urgent Phone Call

Max and Linden followed a squelching Steinberger into the secret elevator that would plunge them through many levels to Harrison's hidden office buried deep within the subterranean bowels of Spy Force. It was a secret elevator because not many people knew about it in the Force, and therefore the world, but also because it was concealed in a series of terra-cotta pots as big as phone booths. Harrison had a real passion for terra-cotta pots, Steinberger had told them. Not all elevators were pots and not all pots were elevators, though, he went on to say, but a simple tap to the side of a pot to test if it was hollow would soon let you know.

Their terra-cotta elevator descended through the many secret levels of Spy Force as a back-to-normal Steinberger chatted on as he would have done in pre-Frond times.

When it came to a stop, a female voice melodiously hoped that they'd had an enjoyable journey and wished them a pleasant stay. Ducking their heads, they made their way out of the potted-plant conveyor to Harrison's floor, leaving the elevator to slip off behind them. Max flicked a clump of dirt from her shoulder and Linden picked a worm from his overalls and returned it to the soil as they took in their surroundings. They were in a plush and opulent foyer full of dark wooden tables and chairs that stood against the walls, reminding Max of starched waiters waiting for instructions. Lining the walls like a stiff-chinned guard of honor was a row of darkened paintings of suited men and women. They were like old portraits of queens, nobles, and rich merchants' daughters, except that all these people had their faces blurred by a colored, misty fog, as when someone's on the news they don't want you to see so they smudge their faces. And at the bottom of each painting were gold plaques with a series of numbers and letters.

"These are paintings of the most accomplished agents who have ever been at Spy Force," Steinberger intoned as if he were leading a tour of Buckingham Palace. "It's our very own Hall of Fame. Of course we can't show their faces. If any of these agents were to be seen by the wrong eyes, there would be ghastly consequences."

Max looked at the blurred faces as she followed Steinberger, who was recounting tales of brave agents and their missions. She stopped in front of one of the paintings.

"Linden?" she said softly. "Does this remind you of anybody?"

"Yeah," he replied seriously. "But I was in a snowstorm at the time so I can't be too sure it's them."

He smiled broadly.

"Look at the ring." Max ignored his joke as Linden leaned in and saw a small ruby ring on the agent's hand.

"Eleanor has a ring like that. So does my mom. My grandma gave identical ones to both of them before she died."

"Maybe it's your mom," he quipped, knowing from all he'd heard about Max's mom that there was more chance of a herd of elephants performing a ballet.

Max gave him a pained whine.

"Okay, so it can't be your mom. But Eleanor?"

"The rings were specially made for them, but if it is Eleanor, why hasn't she ever told us?"

"Maybe because it's someone else," Linden replied. He was finding it hard to picture Eleanor as a spy.

"Maybe." But Max wasn't convinced.

"Coming?" Steinberger stood a little way ahead and stopped to let them catch up.

Their shoes sank into richly textured Turkish carpets—except Steinberger's, which hadn't dried out yet so they were still squishing—and took them past glass cabinets crammed with trophies, awards, medals, relics, letters of gratitude, and keys to various cities around the world.

Max came across a prominently positioned cabinet that held a blue silken cloth. Cradled in the cloth was an ornate, well-thumbed, and important-looking book.

"What's in this one?" she asked.

"Aah." Steinberger placed his hands in front of his face as if he were about to pray. "That is the original Spy Force manual. Written by Harrison's father and grandfather when they founded the agency. It contains the very essence of the Force itself."

Steinberger lost himself somewhere Max and Linden couldn't see.

"But we must get on. So much time and so little . . . No wait, I've done that. Let's just go."

A few steps later, they came to a large wooden door with intricate images of eagles and echidnas carved into it. The eagles made sense, but echidnas? Max was starting to think that sometimes it was better not to ask too many questions.

Steinberger pushed a clump of dampened hair across his forehead and patted down his soggy blue suit in a futile attempt at dewrinkling it. Neither worked to improve his appearance, which had been thoroughly restyled by the Japanese pond.

He stared at his watch. The second hand ticked its way toward twelve.

Slowly.

Max and Linden wondered what they were waiting for.

"Usually when people want to enter these things, they just knock," Max offered.

"Yes, of course." Steinberger nodded, his eyes fixed firmly on the dawdling second hand. "We're almost there."

"Aah," he aahed as the hand pointed to the twelve. "It's time."

He knocked on the door. First two short knocks, then three longer ones, followed by two more quick ones.

"Harrison will see you now. May the Force be with you."

At that he erupted into a throaty, deep-from-the-belly kind of laugh that jounced his tall, lanky body as if he were being dangled at the end of a piece of elastic. A few seconds later, he calmed down and realized that Max and Linden weren't amused.

"It's a bit of a joke here at Spy Force," he tried to explain, but saw that his young companions were unmoved. "Need to attend to my next task. Good luck," he offered seriously and squelched off to his terra-cotta ride.

"I guess we'd better go in," said Max as she reached for the golden doorknob.

The door opened easily and quietly onto a darkened room with a high ceiling and long stained-glass windows. They could just barely make out the sunken leather lounges crowded with cushions, the plush, red-velvet curtains, and the fireplace with its twisted marble sides like bleached candy canes. Covering every measure of wall space were more portraits—their faces still obscured—certificates, awards, accolades, diplomas, the odd tennis racket and fishing rod, and shelves of books that looked like they were clinging to each other to stop from tumbling to the floor. Peppered throughout it all, like out-of-place garden gnomes, were all sizes and shapes of terra-cotta pots.

Max and Linden squinted through the dim light and spied a heavy oak desk in the center of the room. They stepped over a collection of smaller-sized pots and came across a sign on the desk that said THE BOSS.

"Looks like we've got the right place, but where's Harrison?" Linden squinted even harder.

He picked up a copy of Drusilla Knucklehead's crime thriller *Dr. Mullet and the Case of the Missing Toilet*. "I've read this one. Not one of her best. Zoned out on the ending."

Max wasn't thinking about toilets; she was wondering where Harrison might be.

"Maybe he was called away at the last minute on some really important business."

Linden's head filled with other ideas. "Maybe he's foiling the plans of top criminals even as we speak!"

"Maybe he's—" Max's theory was interrupted by a dull thud and a muffled grunt that came from under the desk. She put a finger against her lips in a shhh-like gesture and then, pressing her hands into the green leather top, she leaned over the desk as far as she could.

There was a pause as her puzzled mind tried to catch the words in her head to describe what she was looking at.

"Or maybe he's under the desk with a flowerpot stuck on his head."

A stifled snort wriggled out of Linden's mouth.

"Right. I can see it now. The head of Spy Force under the desk with his head—"

His sentence was cut short by the appearance of a flowerpot rising from underneath the desk. Attached to the flowerpot were the shoulders and body of a man.

"Effuff eee or eye aynge affearance uh ah ab im a mit of fubble," said the flowerpot.

Max and Linden's faces screwed into puzzled stares. Was this some sort of code they were supposed to know? Were they also supposed to take a pot and put it on their heads as a sort of cone of silence to keep their meetings top secret? The arms beneath the pot pointed at the place where a head should be.

"Oou oo eow ee?"

Linden decoded the muffled plant speak.

"I think he's asking for our help."

The pot nodded enthusiastically.

Max and Linden made their way around to the other side of the desk and grabbing hold of either side, tugged at the terra-cotta headpiece.

"One . . . two . . . three . . ." and pulled hard.

The force of the tug pulled the pot away and flung Max and Linden across the room into a clumsily stacked rack of golf clubs.

"Aahh." The man rubbed his head and felt to see if his ears were still attached. "Not a bad job at all. I was conducting an investigation that went a bit wrong. Well done. I'm Harrison, by the way. Don't feel you have to stand so far away. Come closer if you like. Never was one for normalities . . . I mean, *formalities*."

Max and Linden untangled themselves from the clubs and sat down in two huge leather armchairs in front of Harrison's desk.

As Harrison said nothing.

And still nothing.

Linden was curious. "Are we waiting for something?"

"Should be here any minute."

More waiting. Then a knock at the door.

"That'll be them now." Harrison stood up and clapped his hands together in a grand slap. "Now that we're all here, we can sing . . . I mean, *begin*."

Max and Linden turned in their chairs as someone came through the door behind them. As their eyes ran over the guests, two things happened. Max looked like someone who had just sucked on a lemon and Linden's crooked smile became even more crooked. He may have even blushed a little.

"Ella!"

"Linden! They didn't tell me you were going to be here."

"Me either." He blushed even more. "I mean, they didn't tell me you were coming. We got here by invisible jet."

"Invisible jet? I got here by a Sleek Machine. It's a cross between a motorcycle and a glider and moves at an oscillation level that makes it and objects that touch it undetectable to the human eye, unless you wear these special goggles." She pulled a pair of thick-lensed goggles from a jacket pocket. "So you zoom above the cars and buses, and through red lights and no one can stop you."

Steinberger stepped behind a transfixed Linden, whose lopsided smile got shoved over by a look of amazement. "Awesome."

Max watched it all and was trying to come to terms with the fact that her life had taken a disastrous turn for the worst.

"Have you had the tour?" Linden couldn't talk fast enough.

"Yeah. How about the Vibratron 5000?"

"Felt like a fizz frenzy all over me."

"That's what I thought!"

"Feels like one giant puke fest," Max grumbled, unsure how long it'd be before she'd need a lifeboat to save her from all the vomit-gush swirling around her.

"Did you have any Slimy Toadstool?"

"Two helpings," Ella admitted.

"How'd you go on the Wall of Goodness?"

"Passed through without a hitch. It was like falling through a feather cloud."

"Of course it was," Max sneered quietly. "Bet she'd slide straight through a Tunnel of Terror without a scratch too. And a Halo of Hellfire or a Fountain of Fear."

"Oh hello, Max. You're here too. How great!"

Finally Miss Perfect has decided I'm not invisible after all, Max thought. "Hi, Ella." She didn't put too much effort into trying to muster any enthusiasm.

Steinberger had cleared a pile of terra-cotta pots from another chair for Ella as Harrison got the meeting under way.

"I thought it was time to bring my three young flies . . . I mean, *spies* . . . together in London to officially say thank you for thwarting Mr. Blue's evil plans to steal the Time and Space Machine."*

Linden and Ella smiled at each other as Max was thinking of ways to erase the last few minutes of her life and replace them with a different version of events altogether.

One that didn't involve Ella.

"How is the machine going? Ben and Francis finished it yet?" Harrison asked hopefully.

Max hesitated. "There's been a small hitch. They're really busy at the moment and it's going to take a little longer than they thought."

"Never mind. We'll get in contact with them and see what help they need from us. It will revolutionize the world once it's finished. As long as it stays out of Blue's hands, the world will have everything to worry about . . . that is, *nothing* to worry about. We'd also like to offer you something. Steinberger?"

The tall, damp man stepped from behind the chairs and handed them three white scrolls tied with a red ribbon flecked with gold.

*For more exciting details see *Mission: In Search of the Time and Space Machine*.

"Max, would you like to read yours out cloud . . . I mean, *loud?*" Harrison invited her.

She unrolled the parchment and read the message. There was a soft click before some official brass band–type music played quietly in the background.

Dear Max Remy,
For your bravery and services to this country and the world, I, Reginald Bartholomew Harrison, the Chief of Spy Force International Spy Agency, hereby invite you to be inducted into the Force and to carry out the noble and time-honored task of fighting crime and other dastardly acts for the protection of humanity and betterment of the world.
Signed

And following this was a scribbled smudge that looked like a misguided worm had slid through a puddle of ink and left its scrawled mark.

Steinberger reached across and after another click sound, which Max saw was the *stop* button on a tape machine, the music stopped.

"What do you think?" Harrison's eyes lit up like a miniature amusement park and, Max thought, the room seemed to go even dimmer. "The bravery and skill you exhibited in outsmarting Blue are some of the finest examples of, well, bravery and skill we've seen at the Force, and we think you'll make excellent additions to an already highly intelligent network of agents."

Max turned to look at Linden, but he was smiling at Ella who was looking back at him and blushing like some kind of sunburned sea slug.

Harrison continued.

"There'll be times when you'll be incognito at some of the world's richest playgrounds or standing side by side with some of the most sinister human beings to ever get dressed in the mornings. Or times when you'll be facing situations so terrifying, it'll take all your energy just to keep sneezing . . . make that, *breathing*. Danger will become your closest associate, lurking behind you like a black panther. Quiet and dangerous and ready to strike at any second."

As Harrison finished, the lights brightened and Max spied Steinberger at the dimmer switch.

She was stupefied. She was sitting in the headquarters of the world's top spy agency, being asked to become a superspy.

She tried to find a suitable answer to such an important invitation, and cursed in her head when all she could come up with was, "Okay."

Ella and Linden were also in.

"Yeah."

"Sounds great."

"Excrement . . . oops, sorry. I mean, *excellent*. Of course, as Spy Force agents, your identity will remain a secret outside these walls and you will tell no one, not even your closest friends and relatives, of your position. Secrecy is the linchpin of our survival. And once you've been inducted as agents of Spy Force, you're members for life. We just need to get you outfitted, give you your spy pack, and a few others strings . . . make that *things*, and you'll be on your way."

Just then a series of ringing sounds was heard.

"That'll be the phone." Steinberger began looking around the room. "What was it last time, sir?" he asked Harrison.

"Cricket bat, I think. It was the iron the time before that, which could have been nasty if it'd been left on."

Max, Linden, and Ella looked on as the two men checked boxes, lifted papers, and opened cupboards searching for the phone, and every now and then picking up cups, bells, or rulers before saying "Hello."

"Here it is." Harrison picked up a golf ball. He pulled the ball in two halves that were joined by a piece of electrical wire and spoke into it.

"Hello?"

There followed a series of uh-huhs that became more solemn as the call went on.

Steinberger explained the phone situation. "As a security measure, the Central Response Investigative Safety Patrol or CRISP, which is responsible for the internal security of Spy Force, changes the phone system on a regular basis."

"I see," Harrison continued. "We only have one choice then."

He clicked the two ends of the ball together and looked seriously at his three new agents.

"Team, you're about to go on your first mission."

Mission! Max sat up ready to accept her orders.

"As you know, when you courageously uncovered the criminal activities of Blue, he resigned from the Department of Science and New Technologies and went very quiet for a while. Now if there's one thing we've learned about Blue over the years, it's that when he goes quiet, you can bet your right shoe he's up to nothing . . . I mean, *something*."

Harrison came back to the desk and sat importantly in his chair.

"He seemed to have stopped his evil ways and adopted a new public face as the manufacturer of a range of food for kids. He's marketed his foods with much success. Like the Alien Snot Jelly range, which is the number one jelly in the country. Everything looks innocent enough, but Spy Force has uncovered information suggesting that Blue has invented a concoction that, when eaten, controls minds. Now that his foods are so popular, he is going to include the ingredient in his recipes and begin his domination of the minds of children all over the world. We must slop him! I mean, *stop* him. And who better than the three of you to do it. You've seen firsthand how Blue's mind works and as kids you will be the perfect undercover agents for this mission. Of course, you'll need to be in disguise. Since Blue has seen your faces, he will recognize you instantly if he sees you as you are."

"We'll have aliases." Linden pictured himself smartly dressed and walking with the swagger and style of James Bond. Max pictured herself dangling from helicopters, climbing mountains, and parachuting from planes.

"What do we need to do?" asked Ella.

"You will infiltrate Blue's factory, Blue's Foods, and go undercover as . . ." Harrison paused to add dramatic effect, "BRATTs."

Max's shoulders fell.

"Excuse me?"

"BRATTs. Bona-fide Registered Authorized Taste Testers."

"Is that a real job?" Linden became excited.

"It certainly is," Steinberger leaped in to clarify. "There are kids who travel all around the world simply to taste new foods. They're also given tutors to help them study for school as well as complete specified BRATT training courses."

"Why didn't anyone ever tell me about this before?" Linden puzzled. "That's it, I'm switching careers. I know I've only been a spy for about five minutes, but I'm not too big a man to say I made the wrong choice."

Ella giggled as Linden tried for as long as he could to hold the serious pose he'd taken. It didn't last long.

Max stared at both of them, wondering what it would take to have their mission treated a little seriously.

Harrison completed his instructions. "An agent has been placed in the factory as a nude technologist . . . um, excuse me, I mean a fully clothed, *food* technologist and will be your point of contact once inside. Sleek will take you as close as he can to the factory, where another agent will meet you and declothe the rest of the mission details . . . that's, um, *disclose* the details. For now Steinberger will take you to the lab where Quimby will equip you with all the deer you need . . . um, that's *gear* you need, and provide you with your disguises and new aliases."

He rose and stood at attention. Max, Linden, and Ella followed his lead and only just held back an impulse to salute.

"I believe you're the best team for this job and have no doubt that Mission Blue's Foods will be a swift and successful operation. There's just one thing left to say: All systems are go." Harrison raised an eyebrow for emphasis. "Always sounded so good when the *Thunderbirds* said it, so I've borrowed it for Spy Force. Good luck, team!"

With Harrison's words resonating in their ears like the bells of Big Ben, Max, Linden, and Ella followed Steinberger out of the office to be equipped for their first mission as Spy Force agents.

CHAPTER 15

Mission: Blue's Foods

After a cramped ride in another terra-cotta pot, Max, Linden, Ella, and Steinberger arrived at Quimby's lab ready to be equipped for Mission Blue's Foods.

"This is a very special part of the Force. It's the birthplace of many of the inventions that are created here at Spy Force and is run by perhaps one of the most brilliant scientists in this country, maybe the world. Why there's even . . ."

Steinberger was cut off by the sudden appearance of Dretch stealing out of the lab. "Ah, Dretch. Good to see you again. Doing a little maintenance work?"

Dretch flinched and spun around, offering the three new spies a prickly stare as if they'd just run over his favorite pet. With one eye poking out from behind his craggy bangs, they each felt an ice-cold tingle run down their spines that made them want to reach for a long warm coat to stop their blood from freezing over.

"Urrrrr," urred Dretch as he skulked away, his sagging maroon coat only just managing to cling to his hunched shoulders.

"The Hunchback of Notre Dame stands a good chance of losing his job as long as that guy's around," Ella shivered, still trying to shake the icy chill.

"Yeah, and if the Hunchback were ever hard up on cash, he could earn a few dollars giving Dretch a few beauty tips." Linden rubbed his shoulders, trying to get some warmth back into them.

Just then, Delilah burst out from behind the lab door and screeched past Max's nose before landing expertly on all four paws and rushing after her owner.

Max wasn't feeling so amused about Dretch's bad attitude or his cat's sudden appearance. She needed to know more.

"What's wrong with him?" she demanded of Steinberger.

"Dretch? Nothing. He's just got a different way of looking at the world from most people." And then he balked, as if he were trying to figure out how to say the next part. "Sometimes when things go wrong, it can leave people quite . . . changed."

"Did something bad happen to him when he was a spy?"

"Let's just say there's a kind and good man hidden beneath that somewhat rough exterior."

"Any more rough an exterior and he could double as barbed wire," mumbled Linden.

Max wasn't going to let Steinberger off so easily. "But what did he mean when he said others like us have come before and have never been seen again?"

"He said that?"

"Yes. Outside the VART."

"He has an unusual sense of humor not many of us share. Trust me. He'd never mean that."

Steinberger turned away and knocked on the lab door.

"Come in," a small disembodied voice moused from within.

Steinberger led the way inside, but Max wasn't satisfied. That was the second time they'd seen Dretch, and something told her he may not have been in the lab for Spy Force business alone. And how come he was in there just as they were about to get their spy packs? He'd made it clear he didn't want them around and maybe he was planning something to get rid of them sooner. She made a note to keep an eye on Dretch, and was determined to find out what it was Steinberger wasn't saying about him.

The lab was a shining maze of chrome benches, transistors, resistors, circuit boards, cords, wires, diodes, and electrical gadgets that ticked, flicked, and whirred. There were cupboards with glass doors toppling over with jars, tubes, and bottles. There were fridges, burners, beakers, soldering irons, clamps, safety masks, and an enormous fish tank with seaweed, a little stone castle, and a small tropical fish called Fish.

"Team." Steinberger referred to them now as *Team*. "Meet Professor Quimby, the head inventor of Spy Force. She's a professor of physics, astrophysics, chemistry, robotics, and holds the trophy for Spy Force bowling champion three years in a row."

Quimby looked embarrassed.

"A few lucky strikes, that's all."

She looked away and buried her burning-red face in the long wisps of dark hair that fell around her head like a shower curtain. A bright pink scarf tied in a knot at the back of her head struggled to hold the rest of it in some kind of order. She wore a long yellow coat over baggy dark-blue trousers and red and white striped sneakers.

"Before each Spy Force mission, our agents are supplied with packs that have been specially equipped for their particular assignment," Steinberger explained. "It's up to Quimby and the lab staff to read the mission specifications and decide what you may need. They're experts at this and have never been wrong yet. Quimby?"

The scientist's head shot up as if she'd just heard a loud bang.

"Would you like to take our new recruits through their packs?" Steinberger added.

Quimby pushed another snaking piece of hair out of her face with her latex-gloved fingers. In front of her were three backpacks of differing designs and colors.

"We don't have much time. We've been preparing for this mission for weeks and now that it's happening, we've no time to lose. These may look like ordinary bags but they are in fact bottomless. No matter how much you put in them, they will never be full and never heavier than two pounds. Also, if you open the pack completely, it can be spread out so far it can be used it as a coat, a piece of camouflage—it is color-sensitive so that it instantly blends in with your surroundings—or with these strings, even a parachute. It also has a special locking device that is sensitive to your fingerprints. The instant you touch it, the bag will recognize your prints and open only for you."

She held out three booklets called *1001 Uses for a Super Pack*. "All the possible uses and functions of the bag are spelled out in this." She gave them each a copy.

She handed out the booklets, undid the zipper around one of the packs, and opened the front cover to reveal what was inside. Then she picked up a matchbox-size device that looked like a miniature TV.

"This is a Substance Analyzer Meter, or SAM. It can identify almost any known substance in existence. All you need to do is hold the top end of the SAM to the substance you wish to identify, and within seconds a reading of all the components of that substance will appear on this screen along with their level of toxicity or danger."

"Better not put it near one of your jokes or the thing will explode," Linden whispered in Max's ear. Max opened her mouth to shoot off a reply but when she heard the tittering of Ella nearby, she pursed her lips so tightly they resembled the rear end of an uptight cat.

"And this," continued Quimby, blowing an unruly piece of hair from her mouth, "is a Danger Meter. In the presence of danger, it emits an electronic pulse. The stronger the vibrations, the more dangerous the situation. It's best to wear this inside your clothes, so when there's danger nearby, you'll know it instantly."

She then picked up a circular metallic disc and held it carefully in her hand.

"This precious thing moves objects from a distance. Just point the channeling beam at the object you'd like to move, and control the movement of the object with this miniature joystick. It's called the RHINO, or the Remote Hauling Infra-nice Operator.'

"Infra-nice?" Ella queried.

"Yeff," murmured Quimby as her scarf finally failed to hold back her wild hair and fell over her face. "We decided we liked the name RHINO and we couldn't think of another suitable word that started with N."

The professor then handed them each a watch and asked them to put them on.

Linden's was a transparent ice-blue color that showed the components working inside. Ella's was silver with a fliptop cover that revealed a red metallic watchface, while Max's was bright pink with a picture of a pony behind two sparkling watch hands.

"Pink?" she asked in disgust. "I can't wear pink. And what's with the pony?"

"These are walkie-talkie watches," said Quimby timidly.

"I'm sure they are," Max agreed firmly. "But I can't be seen anywhere wearing this. I'll have to have a different one."

"I'm afraid you can't," Quimby reasoned. "Each watch has been specially made for each of you and adjusted to a certain frequency that is suited only to the allocated wearer."

Max knew she couldn't argue against that and wanted to get on with the mission.

"Okay. I'll wear the stupid watch. How do they work?"

"Simply adjust the frequency to the person you wish to speak to and press the side button to begin talking. Max, your frequency is one, Linden on two, and Ella, you're on three."

Quimby reached for another gadget.

"This laser gun cuts through solid metal, this cupcake bomb lets off a silent wall of tear gas, and the truth gum makes the chewer speak nothing but the truth. Everything you have in your packs has been personally checked by me and is in full working order," she finished proudly.

"What do these lollipops do?" asked Linden.

"Nothing. They're just lollipops. A lot of agents have a sweet tooth, so we throw them in as a treat. There are pens and notepads, too, which are also just pens and notepads. And these," said Quimby reaching for three covered coat hangers on a rack nearby, "are your disguises."

Max, Ella, and Linden took their hangers as the sound of zippers being unzipped echoed around the lab.

Quimby continued. "From now on you'll be known as Cynthia, Jeremy, and Angelina."

Max's face screwed into a crunched-up mess as she held out a pink ribboned dress and a long blond wig.

"Don't tell me. I'm Cynthia."

Ella held out a baggy pair of trousers and a bright blue T-shirt. "Which I guess makes me Angelina."

Linden sifted through his bag to find a pair of sneakers, dark denim jeans, and a sports shirt and cap. "Hello there, Jeremy."

Max looked at both of them smiling smugly with their new identities. Of course they'd be happy, she thought, since the whole concept of fashion had managed to pass them by their entire lives. The watch was one thing, but she wasn't going to take the rest of it lying down.

"I don't want to be Cynthia."

"Max, it's just for the mission. Happens all the time in the business." Suddenly Linden was an authority.

"Okay, Mr. Expert. You be Cynthia."

"I'm a boy."

"I'll be Cynthia," Ella volunteered.

Of course, Max thought. *Little Miss Perfect once again acts all nice*.

"I don't want to be Angelina either," said Max, not willing to let Ella win.

All four of them stared at Max.

"After the mission, you'll go back to being Max," Quimby assured her. "But for now your identities are fixed."

Just then Frond billowed through the door, her coat trailing behind her in a red, swirling *whoosh*, and her beehive hairdo half-collapsed like a mini–Leaning Tower of Pisa. Steinberger's face drained of color so much that he almost disappeared in the white glowing lab, except for the beads of sweat that again began dappling his nervous brow.

"Sorry I'm late. I got caught up with an oversized Venus Flytrap that mistook me for lunch. My fault. Should have remembered it was feeding time."

Frond's coat pocket was torn and her sleeve seemed covered in some kind of milky-colored goo. In a blurred daze, Steinberger lifted her hand, which had a few scratch marks and a tiny trickle of blood. He wiped it against his jacket in a smooth, slow gesture but when he realized his hand was holding hers, he let it go instantly and looked very much like he was going to faint.

"I think I might wait outside," he stammered, trying to figure out how to make his feet walk toward the door and tripping over them in the process.

Frond was unphased as she lifted a small cotton pouch onto Quimby's desk.

"I've brought a few Plantorium goodies that may come in handy, like this sneeze powder. It makes people sneeze continuously and, as you know, it's impossible to sneeze and keep your eyes open at the same time. Just throw a little at the person you wish to distract. Great for when you need to make a quick getaway. I've also included a stink bomb for each of you in case you need to clear a room fast or just leave a nasty surprise for someone evil. You'll find a face mask as well to save you from the bomb's smelly wares, and there are a few nature bars from Irene in case you get hungry. Packed full of fruit, vitamins, and minerals."

Then she stopped and smiled proudly. "Good luck, and may the Force be with you."

Max, Linden, and Ella were shown to a series of dressing rooms nearby, where they put on their new outfits. Linden and Ella looked up when Max came out, but before they had a chance to say anything, she stopped them.

"Not one word, okay. Not a smirk, not a giggle. Nothing."

She led the way, walking a little uneasily in her patent-leather shoes and dress that looked like a giant pink marshmallow. She grabbed her pack, said good-bye, and headed out of the lab where they found a calmer and more colorful Steinberger, happy to see the disguises working so well.

"You look . . ." he began.

"Um, it's best not to mention it actually," warned Linden.

"Right. To the Vehicular All-Response Tower," he commanded, like he was leading some kind of cavalry into battle.

A short while later, Steinberger stood in front of them on the long metal deck. Sleek—dressed in brown leather goggles, a cap, and a long, scuffed coat like he was some Second World War fighter pilot—warmed up the engine on the Sleek Machine below. Max, Linden, and Ella stood ready for their journey, thick-lensed goggles hanging around their necks.

"Good luck, team."

Steinberger handed them each their BRATT authorization badges and papers as well as a London street directory. He also gave them some money and three rather large handkerchiefs.

"My grandma always used to say, wherever you go, you'll never be lost if you have a handkerchief, and she hasn't been wrong yet."

He was sounding a little choked up, and tears moistened the corners of his eyes. Max took her handkerchief and hoped he wasn't going to cry. She hated anyone bawling in front of her. It made her feel annoyingly embarrassed and curious as to why people didn't save their tears until they were somewhere other people didn't have to witness them. Especially her.

Sleek made the final adjustments on his machine and wondered what the holdup was.

"Remember, use your watches to stay in close contact and make sure each one of you is safe at all times."

Sleek revved the machine and eyed Steinberger through his goggles, wanting him to get a move on.

"And this is my private line. In case you get into any trouble. Which you won't. I'm sure of it. It's just that—"

The horn blasted from the Sleek Machine as Ella took the slip of paper with Steinberger's number and put it in her pocket.

"Thanks."

"Good luck," he sniffed as Linden and Ella climbed on the back of the motorcycle-like machine and Max sat in the sidecar, pushing her bulging pink dress down to fit it all in.

"May the Force be—"

The rest of Steinberger's farewell was lost in the thunder of the Sleek Machine's departure out of the VART and on to Blue's Foods, where Max, Ella, and Linden would embark on their first Spy Force mission. Apart from the dress, Max knew this would be one of the greatest days of her life, but what she didn't know was that deep inside her pack, a small regular pulsing was being emitted from her Danger Meter. The sound and vibrations of the Sleek Machine meant she felt none of it.

As the Sleek Machine left the VART, a small feline cry came from within a shadowy corner as a clutch of pale bony fingers ran the length of its deep black fur.

CHAPTER 16

Agent 31

After an eventful ride through the skies of London, dodging pigeons, swerving around statues, and only narrowly missing being squashed by a double-decker bus as it entered a low-level tunnel at the same time they did, the Sleek Machine arrived with its four passengers in a small park, on a quiet street.

Max unfolded herself from the sidecar, where she was squashed down so low only her head poked out above the leather cover. This, along with the constant flapping of a stray piece of pink dress in her face, meant that all of the sights she'd heard Ella and Linden shouting about had been hidden from her.

Sleek flung one leg over the machine and, taking care to avoid a large crack in the footpath, stood before his passengers. Like an airline steward on an intercom, he bid them good-bye.

"One-way ride to somewhere in the vicinity of Blue's Foods of the three new recruits complete. Please leave your goggles in the appropriate compartments and make sure you take all your belongings with you. Your contact will be here directly to advise you of your next move. Have a pleasant mission and thank you for flying with Sleek."

His serious face flicked into a wide toothpaste-advertisement grin before it snapped back into being serious again, as though sometime in flying school he'd been advised of the importance of such a grin but hadn't quite gotten it right. Avoiding the crack in the footpath once again, he climbed back onto the Sleek Machine and flew into the afternoon. Within seconds the machine disappeared as the oscillation level for invisibility was reached.

"Some ride, huh?" Ella was pleased that Linden had gotten to try the Sleek Machine.

"Heaps better than I thought."

"I wonder how far it can go? Do you think it could fly all over the world?"

"That'd be awesome!"

Max looked at the two of them and wondered why whenever Linden was with Ella he started talking like he was an overacting presenter on some lame kid's show. The ones that are all teeth and no talent.

"Maybe wondering about how we're going to meet our contact would be a more clever way to use the brain capacities you have?"

Max turned away while Ella and Linden threw each other a shrugged look that said they knew they were in trouble but didn't really care.

"And maybe if you sold your brain to science, they could work out the missing ingredient in having a sense of humor."

"What was that?" Max spun around on her shiny black heels, not quite out of earshot of Linden's quip.

"I said maybe if our contact's nearby, they could figure out where we'll be sitting by our professional demeanor."

He whipped into his bag, pulled out his Danger Meter and began clipping it to the inside of his shirt. He concentrated on redoing his buttons to make sure his meter was properly concealed, but mostly to avoid Max's deadly gaze. Ella clipped hers onto the inside of her waistband, also eager to avoid the Maxvibes that were coming their way.

Max was skeptical, and turned away abruptly to sit on a bench nearby. She looked up to see Ella and Linden talking and laughing as the bright sunny day lit up everything around them. She attached her Danger Meter to the pink satin lining of her dress so that it sat just above her heart. As she made sure it was firmly fastened, she again felt that dull, familiar ache she felt whenever she and her mother moved and she knew she was losing a friend. She looked at the two of them laughing and joking together and wondered why she couldn't be the one standing with Linden having a good time. Ella seemed to have everything: a nice mother, a good sense of humor, and Linden liked her better. If only—

"Psssst."

Max's self-pity was interrupted by what sounded like the hissing of a punctured tire. She held her head still as her eyes roamed the park, trying to spy what it was.

"Pssssssst."

This time the sound was louder, plus it sounded like it was coming from the garbage can beside her.

Linden and Ella continued chatting, oblivious of the hissing can.

"Down here." The hissing had turned into a real voice. Max leaned down into the can to come face-to-face with a person looking back at her.

"Cynthia Gordon?"

For an instant Max was going to say no, but then remembered her ridiculous pink outfit. "Yep, that's me."

"I'm Agent 31. Your first contact for Mission Blue's Foods."

"What are you doing in the can?" She had to ask.

"I'm Spy Force's secret hidden agent. It's my job to relay information to agents from discreet places. On the last mission I was posted in the steampipe of an ocean liner. Got a very warm behind on that assignment, I can tell you. The one before that I was in a fish tank. Good thing I can hold my breath so long. Costs a fortune in dry cleaning bills but it's a steady job and I'm pretty good at it, if I do say so myself."

"How can you fit your whole body in such small places?" Max eyed the barrel-sized can.

"I studied the ancient eastern art of Physical Origami for ten years under one of the Grand Masters. You should see what she could do. Once she got in and out of a teapot in ten minutes flat. The tea tasted a bit funny after that, but it was amazing to see."

Max wondered if Agent 31 had mashed a few brain

cells out of existence, and whether his squashed-up experiences had left him a bit nutty.

"And I'm not nutty. I know that's what you're thinking because I also study mind-reading by correspondence. The ancient wisdoms of the world are mysterious and wonderful."

Ella and Linden noticed Max leaning into the can and hurried over.

"Are you okay, Cynthia? Are you feeling sick?" Ella looked concerned.

Max disliked Ms. Perfect even more because she could still be nice even after Max had been rude to her.

"This is Agent 31. He's our contact."

Ella and Linden stared at each other seeing no one around except Max.

"I think you're getting a little too much sun," Linden suggested.

"Just look in the can."

They leaned over the rim and spied a crumpled man.

"Pleased to meet you. Thirty-one's my name and information's my game."

There really was a man in the can.

"What do you have for us?" Max had her notepad ready to take down everything she needed to know. Agent 31 began his instructions.

"In the last three months, Blue's Foods has come to dominate the kids' food business with his fancy new food flavors and marketing campaigns. His latest promotion even offered a trip to the moon to a lucky consumer of his Man in the Moon Cheesy Nibbles. You can imagine how many people bought those little cheesy treats. Anyway, now that so many kids are hooked on his foods, he is planning to add a secret ingredient over the next few months that will slowly take over the minds of kids everywhere, leaving him in control. Your mission is to enter Blue's Foods as a BRATT—a Bona-fide Registered Authorized Taste Tester—find out the ingredient he is planning to use, and stop him before he can have his wicked way. But remember, it's not certain when Blue will start putting his plan into action, so whatever you do, don't eat the food."

Max busily scribbled down all that 31 was saying.

"Your next step is to go to the lawns of Blue's Foods, where you will be ushered along to the food-tasting area. Here is the address and a map of the factory layout for each of you. We believe Blue's office is located here." He reached past an empty potato chip packet and a half-eaten sandwich to point to a particular location on Max's map.

"Once settled into your position, you will contact an agent who has been working undercover as a food technologist. She is of medium build, has long dark hair, and is expecting your arrival. When you see her, you need to say this line, 'The bluebird sings a happy song,' and she'll reply, 'Only when the sparrow farts.'"

Ella and Linden stifled their giggles as Max quickly scribbled the message.

"Good luck and may the Force—"

"Be with you . . . We know." Max stood up from the bench and took the London street directory from her pack.

"Thanks, Agent 31," Ella said, trying to make up for Max's rude behavior.

He smiled warmly. "Call me 31."

"Will we see you again, 31?" asked Linden.

"Perhaps."

"Got it." Max had her finger on the location of Blue's factory. "Let's go."

"Remember," warned 31 before they left. "Watch out for Blue. No matter how nice he may seem, he's one of the meanest characters in the business. And even though you're the perfect agents for this mission, he'll have his eye out for you, so don't do anything that will draw attention to yourselves."

The three of them moved off with the agent's warning circling in their heads. As their feet sank into the soft green carpet of grass beneath them, Max and Linden remembered the vulturelike look of satisfaction on Blue's face as they had dangled perilously over his vat of jelly.* He was a man who'd stop at nothing to get what he wanted, and they'd have to watch every step to keep out of his way.

*For more exciting details see
Mission: In Search of the Time and Space Machine.

CHAPTER 17

Meeting the Undercover Agent

Chronicles of Spy Force:

Alex Crane looked over the rim of her thick tortoiseshell glasses, and held up the Substance Analyzer Meter, or SAM, in front of her.

"Just as I thought."

The reading was the final piece of proof that Blue was up to no good and if she didn't act quickly, he'd launch one of the most evil plans of mind control the world had ever known.

"Now, to get this back to the lab." But before she could take a step, Blue's sniveling henchman, Kronch, snatched the SAM from her and threw it to the floor, smashing it into a million pieces.

"I knew there was somethin' fishy about you. The head technologistician said she wasn't convinced you were just any food technologist, and guess what, she were right."

Kronch paused for effect.

"Ms. . . . Alex . . . Crane."

Alex flinched on hearing her name punctuated by this meat-brained, no-necked half-giant. Kronch was three times her size but had the brainpower of a rock. In a one-arm swoop, he picked up Alex and strode toward the boiling cauldron of Vampire Blood Syrup.

"In just a few seconds, Ms. Crane, you'll turn from superspy to super dessert. Kids all over the world will be slurping you up with their favorite vanilla ice cream and not even know it."

Kronch held Alex over the boiling copper tub as the bubbling, sugary heat rose up and stung her nose and eyes. Kronch wasn't smart, but he was every inch as mean as his uncle Theolodious Blue. Every inch as . . .

"Oooph!" Alex Crane was jolted from Max's thoughts and was replaced by the back of Ella's head right up against her nose.

"Oops. Sorry, Cynthia."

Max boiled.

"Don't stop so suddenly next time and maybe we'll all manage to get to where we're going in one piece."

Max was her own mini-storm as she thundered past Ella toward the factory.

"Don't worry about Max," Linden tried to comfort a downcast Ella. "She has a really nice personality, she just sometimes forgets to bring it with her."

There was no doubting who the factory belonged to. The building was a blazing modern kaleidoscope of glass and curves and colors gleaming in the sun like a mirage in a desert. Outside the factory was like a circus ground with splashes of red, blue, pink, and yellow snuggled among leafy green trees filled with exotic birds and colorful butterflies buoyed on a calm, gentle breeze. Dotted around like giant marbles were statues of rounded chefs holding cartons of custards, stirring pots of puddings, and juggling jars of jelly beans. Towering above everything was a fountain of fake juice spilling from a gigantic mouth and a bold and friendly sign that read, "Blue's Foods . . . So good it's almost criminal."

"I'll bet it's criminal." Max stood under the sign and thought about Ben, Eleanor, and Francis and what Blue had done to them. "We'll get you yet."

A sprawl of kids were arriving for the taste testing, and after hugs and good-byes and adults wiping corners of eyes with handkerchiefs, the BRATTs drifted into two lines. Ella waited in one as Linden stood behind Max in the other.

"The food tasting title they gave us is just a name, you know. You don't actually have to become one," he leaned into her.

"I'm not being a BRATT, but thanks for pointing it out. I just think she shouldn't have stopped so suddenly."

"Ella's really nice, and if you'd just give her a chance, you'll find that too."

Max spun around. "Who said anything about Ella? It's not Ella I'm worried about. I've hardly even noticed Ella. It's the mission I'm worried about, not Ella."

By the amount of times Max said her name, he knew the problem was definitely Ella. Linden sighed. One day he'd understand girls, but today he wasn't even going to get close.

A large truck of a man sitting behind a desk at the front of the line lifted his head to see what the commotion was. He eyed Max closely as she approached the desk and stepped into his darkened shadow. She felt her Danger Meter tingle inside her dress as her eyes rose warily up his bulky frame. He had stubby sausagelike fingers, arms as thick as an old lounge chair, a crumpled orange shirt stretched over his bulging belly, and a bucket-sized head rimmed with a motley black and gray beard that was so thick you couldn't see his lips.

"Badge and papers?" the beard rustled.

Max reached in and took them out of her bag. The way the man was looking at them she wasn't sure he could read. Then she saw something else. Her eyes flung open like window blinds as she read his nametag: "Kronch."

"Kronch?" She didn't realize she'd said it out loud.

"Hmm?" Kronch hmmed grumpily.

"Nothing." Max felt like all the words had been sucked out of her head as she remembered her Alex Crane story.

"First-timer, eh? Just do as the other BRATTs here do and you won't get into any trouble . . . Cynthia." He said her name like he wasn't convinced it was hers.

Kronch looked down at a list in front of him. "Room B for you." He gloated like it was some kind of punishment. Before he let her go he groaned, "Wait, let me see that bag."

Max stiffened. If Kronch saw what was inside her

backpack, they were done for. She tried to think of how to explain her way out of it.

"There's not much in there, just a few—"

"The bag." This time it wasn't a request as much as a quietly spoken threat.

Max took her bag off her shoulders and handed it over. Linden's mouth went dry as he felt his temperature go up.

Kronch was enjoying every minute of their squirming, but when he tried to undo the bag, he got nowhere. He pulled at the zippers, tugged at the straps, and then used his teeth to try and tear it open. Max made a mental note not to touch the bag where his slobber would have sunk in. The security system worked. It seemed the backpack really was meant for no one except Max.

Unable to open it, Kronch threw it to the floor. He moved his beard closer to Max so she could feel his warm, stale breath pouring all over her.

"I'll be keeping a careful eye on you, missy. Make one move out of line, and I'll be on you quicker than a rabbit trap."

Max stepped aside and picked up her pack, unable to take her eyes off the hulking man. Linden stepped up and handed his papers over. He felt his Danger Meter shiver inside his shirt as well. There was something about Kronch that was like rolling black storm clouds after a hot and humid day. Everything was calm now, but any minute the skies were going to open up and come crashing down all over them.

"Room F." Max was sure Kronch was smiling underneath his beard as he ordered Linden to a separate room.

They sidled away from the desk eager to get away from him as soon as possible. Kronch kept them in sight and spoke slyly into a cell phone that looked like a domino in his baguettelike fingers. Ella met them on the neatly manicured lawn near a statue of a large jolly chef holding up a can of whipped cream.

"I'm in Room B," she announced, hoping Linden would be there too.

"Room F," he said disappointedly. "You're with Max."

Ella's smile faltered a little.

"We'll have to make sure we keep in touch with our watches."

Max did her best to ignore Ella's disappointment and turned to walk toward the factory entrance, but as she did, a strap on her pack got hooked on the thumb of the jolly chef and she was flung back into him like a ball on a piece of elastic.

Linden and Ella did their best not to smile but, worried they were going to burst out laughing, moved off quickly. Behind them, Kronch finished his phone call, stood up, and ambled through an oval side door painted like a giant strawberry.

Once inside, Linden said good-bye and was led down

a long polished corridor with glass floors. He could see down into the level below to an organized arrangement of benches, stools, charts, and bowls of brightly colored foodstuff.

Ella and Max were led in the opposite direction. Max's Danger Meter was only now quieting down after her encounter with Goliath. Ella saw her anxious face and guessed what she was thinking. "I don't like being separated from Linden either."

That was exactly how Max was feeling but she wasn't going to let Ella know she was right. "The reason I'm worried is that my Danger Meter doesn't like the hulk we just met one bit. I think it's good we've been split up. We'll cover more ground that way."

"Oh."

"For now let's concentrate on not doing anything that attracts attention."

Just as Max finished saying this, she tripped over another BRATT who had bent over to tie his shoelace. She rolled over the top of him and landed on a skateboard that sped down the polished glass floor, past a forest of kid's legs before she crashed headfirst through the door of Room B, straight into the boots of Kronch.

"Can't you use a door like everyone else?" His nostrils flared like a crazed horse about to bolt. "Now find your seat and do the job you're here to do."

The door opened and other BRATTs giggled as they

stepped over Max. She struggled to her feet, rubbed her sore head, and walked to her allocated desk.

Three food technicians in long white coats with clipboards and pens were pushing carts with different-colored bowls of food. Red, yellow, aqua, and fluorescent pink mousses, custards, jellies, and breakfast cereals. As they approached each desk, they handed over a few bowls and a piece of paper for each BRATT to fill out once they'd tasted their samples.

"Do you think one of these is our contact?" Ella breathed quietly.

"Not sure." Max tried to catch the eyes of each of them. One technician was a short squat man with no hair and a moustache so thin it looked like he had drawn it on with a pencil. Another was a tall woman who chewed gum and wove through the desks nodding her head like she had a radio playing inside it. The final one was very serious, wore thick-rimmed glasses and her long brown hair was tied back in a ponytail. Max had the feeling they'd met before. But how could that be? This was only her second time in London. The technician looked up and caught her eye. She pushed the cart toward Max and stopped alongside her to pick up several bowls and place them in front of her. There wasn't any obvious sign she was their contact, but something told Max she was the one. She looked down, started to fill out her form and decided to give the signal.

"The bluebird sings a happy song."

The technician finished placing Max's bowls on her desk and stepping between the two new spies, did the same for Ella. Max was disappointed. She was sure the contact was her.

The technician held her clipboard up in front of her face and whispered toward Max, "Only when the sparrow farts."

Max pressed so hard on her pencil she snapped the lead.

"Cynthia?"

Max and Ella looked at each other.

"That's me."

"I'm your contact. Crane. Alex Crane."

Alex kept looking at her clipboard and marking off the food samples she'd given them as Max was dealing with a serious case of shock.

"Who?"

"Alex Crane," she repeated softly, barely moving her lips.

Max couldn't believe it. Alex Crane really existed! And she was standing beside her! On the same mission!

"I'm Max!" she almost yelled, plunging her overexcited hands across the desk and sending several bowls of blue and red food samples dribbling onto Alex's coat and trousers.

Kronch's head spun toward them.

Max's embarrassment made her heart beat faster and

her face fire up like she was sitting way too close to a heater.

"Yes, I know . . . Cynthia," replied Alex, annoyed at Max's clumsiness and at revealing her real name. She took a cloth off her trolley and wiped the gunk from her clothes. Max was mortified and desperately wished there was some way she could rewind the last few minutes of her life and start them all over again.

Alex handed out new samples and leaned into them both, pretending to explain the food-tasting process. Kronch stared at them. His eyes like hungry sharks.

"Harrison's information was right. Blue is planning to add a secret ingredient to his food products. One that isn't marked on the package. Which isn't surprising. Half the time you read the ingredients on products and you still don't know what you're eating. Flavor enhancers, colorings, preservatives."

Alex was starting to sound like Max's mother.

"What does this secret ingredient do?" asked Ella, not suffering from any of Max's shock or embarrassment.

"It's called T3-35A. It surrounds the part of the mind that determines good from bad and stops it from working, much like an antibiotic around bacteria, leaving the evil side of a person's mind to take over. It can make an ordinarily good person become evil almost instantly."

Kronch was getting suspicious at how long Alex had been with Max and Ella.

"Meet me in Lab X in an hour and we can take a reading with your SAMs. I couldn't bring mine because of the rigorous search procedures for employees."

"Any problems here?" Kronch's breath floated over them like blackened smog. Max's Danger Meter vibrated inside her dress even harder than before.

"No. They're all set now." Alex put her clipboard on her cart and walked away.

"Harrumph," Kronch harrumphed as he walked back to his desk.

"We've got to tell Linden," Ella whispered.

"Yep," said Max, managing to speak again. "But we've got to get Igor off our backs first. When he's lost interest in us, we'll sneak out of here, get a reading of the secret ingredient, and head back to Spy Force."

Max and Ella pretended to go about their tasting, careful not to put the food in their mouths. In her head Max saw herself knock over the bowls again and again and each time it happened, she became even more angry at herself for being such a klutz. She looked up and saw Kronch speaking furtively into his phone, like he was planning something devious. Something that probably was going to be bad for her. She hoped he would leave them alone, but with the impression she'd made on him so far, she knew that wasn't going to happen easily.

CHAPTER 18

A Terrible Double-cross

After half an hour of food testing, the BRATTs were given a short break to refresh their tastebuds with Blue's Foods Fresh-from-the-Spring Mineral Water. The glass-floored corridor filled with a frenzied clutch of kids drinking water and talking food samples, as Max and Ella stood as far away as they could, trying to figure out what to do.

"Kronch is watching us so closely there's no way we're going to be able to sneak away and meet Alex," Ella deduced.

"You noticed." Max was chewing a fingernail and not trying one bit to be nice to her.

"What do you think we should do?"

"I think you should be quiet, so I can figure that out."

Max skated over some ideas in her head, wondering why, of all the places in the world, she had to share the part she was in with Ella.

"I've got it! *We* can't sneak away, but Linden might be able to."

Max put her hand to her chin, adjusted the frequency on her watch and began talking.

"Come in, Lin . . . I mean, Jeremy. It's . . ." Max could hardly say it, "Cynthia. Can you hear me?"

"Loud and clear," came a tinny, wire-thin voice from her watch.

"Good. We've got a plan—"

"It's no good," interrupted the voice.

"What do you mean it's no good? You haven't heard it yet."

"It's me, Angelina."

"What?" Max turned around and saw Ella with her watch to her mouth.

"Jeremy is frequency two."

"I knew that." Max hated being wrong and hated even more being *told* she was wrong. "My frequency button must be stuck."

Kronch came out of Room B and stood at the door, his eyes carving into them like chain saws tearing through wood.

Max tried to ignore her Danger Meter and turned her back on Kronch as she spoke into her watch as discreetly as she could.

"Jeremy, are you there? We've got proof that Blue is up to no good. Jeremy? Can you hear us?"

Nothing. Max tried again.

"Can you hear us, Jeremy? We need your help."

"Ah, how I've missed that voice. So lovely to hear from you again." Max's heart jolted in her chest like it momentarily forgot how to keep beating. "I was just on the phone to Kronch who was telling me how lucky we are to have you with us . . . Ms. Maxine Remy."

It was Blue.

And he had Linden's watch.

Which meant he must have Linden.

"Your little game, Maxine, while brave, has unfortunately come undone and, as you know, in this business, that sadly comes with unpleasant consequences." He paused. "And perhaps some bad news for your little friend Linden."

At the mention of Linden's name, Max felt a wave of fury crash through her. If Blue hurt him in any way she'd do everything she could to make him regret it. Her finger pressed hard on the talk button to let him have it. "Now listen, Blue—" but before she could say anything further, the watch went dead.

Hearing Blue's voice again struck deep fear into her as if she were sailing toward a hidden iceberg lurking dangerously in frozen waters. When she tried to swallow, it felt like an icy lump was stuck in her throat and, what was worse, when she looked up, she saw Kronch heading straight for them.

"Quick! Run!" she yelled.

"Where?" Ella asked.

"Not sure. Just run."

They raced along the corridor followed by a lumbering Kronch. He pushed past a group of BRATTs, sending them hurtling into fake jelly baths and gloopy mountains of imitation cheese. People below looked up as Max's and Ella's legs hurled them as fast as they could across the glass floor toward a huge twisting banana slide that connected their floor to the one below. They looked behind them and saw Kronch gaining on them.

"Down there," Max instructed before leaping onto the

slide and plunging around the yellow twists and turns and landing headfirst in the soft belly of an armchair shaped like a chef.

Max just managed to get out of the way as Ella nose-dived into the pudgy lounge.

"Lucky you were here," she breathed at the chef, pulling her curls out of her face.

"Urrrr."

Ella's eyes rocketed wide open as she thought the chair spoke back to her, but, looking up, they saw it was Kronch, trying to lift his oversized body onto the banana slide. They considered each of the four corridors around them.

"Which one do we take?" Ella thought they all looked the same.

Kronch had managed to get one leg on the slide.

"This one," Max decided and they sped off down the closest one.

They flew past bulletin boards filled with posters of happy kids eating and laughing, and cabinets filled with award-winning Blue's Foods products. They ran so that each step was faster than the one before, until they came to an abrupt stop at a solid steel door.

Kronch's broken cry foghorned behind them as he toppled down the slide.

Gulping big drafts of air, Max tried the door.

"It's locked."

A bellowing cry sounded behind them as Kronch

missed the armchair and whacked straight into the concrete wall behind it.

"My Danger Meter is going crazy," Ella breathed.

Then Max had an idea.

"The laser!" She reached into her pack, took the device from its hold and pointed it toward the lock. She pressed hard on the detonator button knowing this would be their only chance to get away from the fast-approaching Kronch, but when her finger came to a stop, she stared at the small gray gadget, trying to believe what she saw.

Nothing had happened. She pressed the detonator button again and again but still there was nothing. Quimby's words zigzagged in her head. The ones that told her all their gadgets had been checked and were in full working order. What were they going to do now?

Ella inhaled a quick fear-filled breath as Kronch got closer and closer. She took her laser from her pack and aimed it at the door.

"It's worth a try," she explained, wishing as hard as she could that her laser would work.

She pressed the button hard and a sharp line of red light blasted a high-powered beam at the lock.

"It works!" she cried.

Kronch's plodding footsteps got closer and closer as the smell of melting steel filled their noses.

"Quick," Max pleaded as the laser drew a heated line

around the lock, leaving a puddle of liquefying mess at their feet.

Kronch was so close they could hear his labored grunting as his stale breath clamored to escape his lungs.

Ella held the laser firm, aiming it directly at the lock, as Max's mind raced back to when they had collected their packs and to the last person she had seen just before they had entered the lab. *Dretch!* Of course. It was obvious he hated them and would get rid of them if he had the chance. He must have slipped into the lab to sabotage her laser before she picked it up. Which means he must be a double agent. That would explain why he flinched when he heard Harrison's name. They were in deep trouble now, but if they didn't get back to Spy Force soon, the very existence of the agency was in serious danger.

"Please!" Just as Max said this, the lock fell to the floor and the door creaked open.

"All right!" they cheered before Kronch's thumping footsteps cut their celebration short.

Max took off through the door and skidded around a corner where she spied a dumbwaiter in the shape of two bulging red lips.

"In here!" She parted the lips and Ella ducked inside with Max following quickly after her. She pressed the *down* button and, pulling her hand quickly inside, the machine began its descent, just as an enraged Kronch reached the top of the shaft and shouted down to them.

"You won't get away from me that easily, you brats."

The words rained on them like a volley of poisonous darts.

Max took the map of the factory out of her pack. "If my guess is right, Linden is being held in Blue's office."

"According to the CTR, he's somewhere much closer than that." Ella held the device in her hand and tried to estimate his position.

Max rolled her eyes. "Or somewhere nearby, which I was going to say before you interrupted."

"What will we do when we find them?" Ella was still nervous about Kronch's menacing threat.

"I don't know. We can figure that out on the way."

Ella wasn't so sure that was the best thing to do. "Don't you think we should figure out a plan before we sneak up on one of the most evil masterminds in the world?"

Max looked up from her map and offered Ella a stare so icy it could have kept a packet of peas frozen for a month. "We've got to get moving now or there'll be none of Linden left to save."

Then, just because she could be nasty, she added, "Unless saving yourself is more important."

For the first time ever, something snapped inside Ella and she decided she'd had enough of Max's constant bad attitude.

"You think you're always so right, don't you, Ms.

Expert dot-com? I don't know who told you your brain is superior to everyone else's but if I were you, I'd trade it in for a new one because the one you've got is a real reject."

Max's head jerked back, as she wasn't sure she was hearing right.

Ella was just getting warmed up.

"And another thing, Miss Crabby, it's obvious you don't have many skills as a people person, but you could at least try and scrape together a little decency so you're a bit more pleasant to be around."

Max was dumbfounded. She'd never heard Ella speak like this before. Part of her was stunned that Ella could get so angry, but the other part of her had to hand it to her. That was a good piece of insulting.

"Linden's right." Ella stuck her chin out and raised one eyebrow. "You need to take yourself shopping for a badly needed dose of humor."

The dumbwaiter came to a halt and the hatch opened in front of them.

Max knew Linden didn't think she had such a great sense of humor. That was okay. She could handle not being very funny, but there was something about hearing it from Ella that really hurt. When she tried to think of something to say, the only thing she could come up with was, "Oh, yeah?"

"Yeah," Ella said defiantly.

She bent her head and walked through another set

of lips into a large, brightly lit basement. It was crammed with shiny metal cylinders mounted on tall, spindly legs that looked like gigantic, overweight insects. Steam was rising from their heads and the sound of bubbling echoed from inside them like hunger pains.

Ella crossed her arms in front of her and stared at Max, daring her to say more.

"At least I'm taking this mission seriously," Max began. "Unlike you, who is so caught up with looking pretty that you—"

"What's going on?" a voice nearby asked.

"Wait your turn," Max snapped, resenting the interruption and continuing with Ella. "You're so caught up with looking pretty . . ."

Max stopped and spun around.

"Linden!" she squealed as she threw her arms around him in a very unMax-like manner. "We were so worried about you. Where have you been? Are you okay?"

Linden laughed and pried Max's tight grip from his neck.

"There's no need to get all gushy. I was only in a different lab."

Shocked at her overemotional reaction, Max straightened her dress and tried to find something else to do with her hands. She lowered her voice a few octaves. "We thought you were with Blue."

"Why would I be with Blue?" he asked.

"He was speaking on your watch," Ella told him.

"I must have dropped it somewhere," Linden said a little sheepishly, patting down what was for him an immaculately neat hairdo.

"That's weird," Max puzzled. "My Danger Meter is buzzing."

"The whole place down here is full of bad energy. This is where Blue is planning to add the secret ingredient," Linden added a little too quickly.

"How do you know that?" Ella questioned.

"Well, where else would they do it? This is the main food preparation area if you look on the map."

While Linden looked like Linden, except for the hair, there was something very unLindenish about him.

"Guess who our contact is?" Max suddenly remembered.

Linden seemed annoyed. "You've met her already?"

"Yep. It's Alex Crane!"

She expected a big reaction but got none.

"You know. Alex Crane. From my book." She was disappointed. Linden was the only one who'd read the Alex Crane adventures she'd written. Apart from Toby and the kids he read to at school while she was in the mud.

She checked her watch. "We've arranged to meet her in Lab X in five minutes." To try and hide her disappointment at Linden's lack of enthusiasm, she concentrated on the map. "According to this, it's on the second floor—"

"Don't worry about the map. I know a shortcut," Linden cut in, not showing the least bit of curiosity at the fact that Alex Crane was real.

Ella threw an inquisitive glance at Max, who for the first time since they'd met, felt the same way as she did. They walked warily behind him through the spindly insect legs, beneath the rumbling metal stomachs, and onto a conveyor belt that wound its way up and over, in and around the whole churning super kitchen. It then began a steep climb high into the extractor fan-filled ceiling.

Max was worried. There was something very odd about the way Linden was behaving. Normally he would have been excited about meeting Alex. He wouldn't have minded her throwing her arms around him. He would have asked more questions about where they'd been. Especially of Ella. And the final clue that made her think something was wrong: He hadn't made one joke since they'd found each other.

"Here we are," he announced as he hopped off the conveyor belt in front of a furry blue door surrounded by blue frosted windows.

"Are you sure this is it?" Max was expecting something very different of Lab X.

"Yep. Come inside," Linden offered as if he were inviting them into his own home.

He opened the door and stood aside as they moved into a dark, silent room.

"I'll get the light."

They heard a click followed by the gentle infusing of soft light that revealed a totally blue room. Blue beanbags, blue floor covered by blue rugs, blue televisions, a blue fridge, and a blue desk. There were even blue plants growing out of blue soil.

"This doesn't look like a lab." Ella's Danger Meter was going berserk.

"That's because it isn't." They turned to see a figure at the top of a blue staircase with a thick, blue snake coiled around the railing.

It was Blue.

He moved down the stairs with catlike grace. Kronch stood at attention beside a molded blue desk swathed in the light of a blue, jelly bean–shaped lamp.

"Welcome, little ones. We're so happy to have you with us."

"Well, don't get used to it," Max warned him, "because we aren't staying." As she turned to go, the door slammed shut, courtesy of a remote control clamped in Kronch's lumpy hand.

"What'll we do now?" Ella whispered to her friends. Before anyone could answer, something happened that even today can still make Max's blood turn to ice.

Linden looked at them, smiled, and walked slowly over to stand next to Blue.

"Linden?" Max wasn't sure what was happening, but

deep inside her she knew it wasn't good.

"Mr. Blue and I have been chatting." Linden's voice was slow and deep, like a talking doll when the batteries are running low. "He has convinced me that what he is doing here at Blue's Foods is for the good of humanity and Spy Force is only trying to stop that."

A smile crawled up Blue's face like a spider climbing toward a fly trapped in his web. Slow. Dangerous. Ready to devour.

Normally Linden had a body that leaned with a kind of slouch and wild hair that even heavy-duty cement couldn't tame. The Linden standing next to Blue looked like he'd been stretched out on a rack, made five inches taller, and had hair so smooth and slick, it looked like one solid, glistening piece.

"You now have two choices," he continued, like he was some overpaid businessman about to bankrupt a small country and enjoying every minute of it. "You can join us and help the struggle of Blue against the unprogressive and selfish workings of Spy Force, or . . ." and at this he paused, sneaking Blue a devoted glance, "you can enjoy the one-way thrill ride of the Moons of Mars confectionery room."

Kronch let out a strangled snort.

Max and Ella felt like someone had wrenched them out of their lives and dumped them into a world they didn't understand.

Nothing was familiar.

Nothing made sense.

Linden not only agreed with Blue, he was now one of his most loyal supporters.

CHAPTER 19

A Sticky End

The Moons of Mars confectionery room was filled with a highway of bright-red conveyor belts going in all directions and large, rounded cauldrons filling the air like oversized silver balloons. The cauldrons were labeled CHOC-COOKIE MIXTURE, TOFFEE-CARAMEL, and SPRINKLES. Each of the machines was churning away, like a mechanical army pouring, sprinkling, and slicing to a rhythmic, ordered beat, busily making the confectionery delights. The machine that had everyone's attention was the one in the center, where two securely bound prisoners were about to become part of the cookie-making process.

Max and Ella hadn't accepted Linden's offer of joining the ranks of Blue's Foods. In fact, Max had been so opposed to it, she had suggested that Linden take the offer and put it somewhere that sounded really painful. As a result of her blunt suggestion, Max's and Ella's backpacks had been removed and they'd been tied up with rope and tossed onto one of the conveyor belts like sausages on a barbecue.

Framed by stacks of large cotton bags filled with choc-cookie mix and sprinkles, industrial ovens, mixers, temperature gauges, rising steam, and pipes that ran around the room like long fingers hugging the walls, Linden picked up a finished cookie from a rack nearby and took a small bite. Again this was unlike Linden, who would have finished the chocolate mound in one swift munch.

"At the moment, with everyone having minds of their own, the world's in a complete mess." He took another careful nibble. "I mean, look at it. We've got wars, famine, poverty, environmental collapse, banks, overpopulation. If only we had one unified way of thinking, the world would be without chaos and hatred for the first time in the history of mankind."

"Humankind," Max corrected.

Blue stood behind Linden, his hands held snugly across his chest, proud of his newest recruit and enjoying every minute of the crumbling friendships before him.

Linden finished the last of his cookie. "You're too cute, Maxine."

He knew Max hated being called that. She clenched her teeth so hard, she only just avoided chipping them.

Ella stared at the boy who was once her good friend but who was talking like someone she normally tried hard to avoid.

"You don't really believe that, do you?" she asked quietly. "What about all that stuff we found out about Blue last time?"

"Ella," Linden said with as much condescension in his voice as it could hold. "At your age and with your intelligence, have you never heard of bad press?"

"Bad press!" Max shouted. "Spy Force is made up of the good guys and you know it."

"Don't talk to me about Spy Force!" Blue shouted, his hands falling from his chest into two closed fists. "They're the ones who can't recognize good from evil."

Max stared at the unusually flustered and rouge-colored Blue.

"It is they who walk around pretending to be the good guys and pointing fingers at the bad guys when they haven't the least idea."

Max watched Blue's chest lurching in and out as if he'd just run a marathon. A sprig of normally perfect hair fell in front of his face, which had become distorted with anger. Max frowned as she tried to figure out what she'd said that had upset Blue so much. Then she had it. It was something Steinberger had said to her at the Wall of Goodness.

"You were the Spy Force agent who went bad, weren't you?" She said it through a small, quiet gasp.

Blue pounced forward and slammed his fist onto the conveyor belt beside Max's head. He was so close to her, she could feel his rage trembling inside him.

"It wasn't me who went bad. It was them!" The fury in his eyes lit the edges of his face with a dangerous glow. "It was I who had the ideas to turn Spy Force into an organization to be reckoned with. We could still do the good deeds they wanted but with a few clever deals of mine, they could have had vast reserves of money to solve any crime they'd wanted. But they wouldn't listen." Blue's face crumpled into an ugly sneer. "Harrison's do-gooding ways blinded him from seeing that what I was saying made perfect sense. We were a good team, Harrison and I, before he threw it away."

Max knew she should have been scared, but she couldn't hold back a widening grin.

"So they threw you out of the Force?"

Blue's eyes fixed on her malevolently like she was a target he was sighting. "They didn't throw me out; I quit," he said in a voice that moved over her like a cold wind.

Just then, the door of the confectionery room crashed open and a bound, gagged, and struggling Alex Crane was hauled in by the bumbling, lumpish Kronch.

"Alex?" Max's head spun around to see her hero being carried in like a bag of potting soil.

"Ah, you found her, Kronch. Well done." Blue straightened himself up, pushed his momentarily unruly hair into place, and went back to being his usual composed and evil self. "Where was she?"

"On her way here, looking for these kids. But I nabbed her before she got too close."

Alex flinched in his grip, desperate to release herself from his leaden hold.

"That's the most intriguing part about most humans," Blue puzzled, now back in control of his behavior. "They have this terrible weakness for other people. They build up all these emotions and loyalties. Terribly icky stuff that just gets in the way of life. It's such a design fault. If I was in charge of designing humans, that would be the first thing to go."

Kronch hardly moved as Alex squirmed and moaned

through her gag. Linden smiled as Blue continued outlining his devilish plan.

"Don't worry, Ms. Crane. Kronch is about to help you get your wish of joining your young friends. Kronch?"

The oversized oaf nodded his bucket head and dragged Alex to the conveyor belt. After a brief struggle, she was securely tied to the belt between Max and Ella.

"Take her gag off," Blue ordered. Kronch did as he was told as a smile filled with meanness etched into Blue's lips. "Comfortable, Ms. Crane?"

"I've never been comfortable in the presence of snakes," she shot back.

Max smiled. Her hero was every bit as clever as she'd written.

"Now, now, Ms. Crane. I don't think there's any need for insults."

"That was no insult, Blue. It was the best compliment I could give you."

Blue's smiled slipped a little, then he quickly regained his composure.

"Now that the whole gang is here, the Moons of Mars coating process can begin and we can be rid of three very pesky obstacles to making the world a better place. And this time I am going to stay and watch," he said, remembering the time Linden and Max had given him the slip. "Linden? Would you do us the honor?"

Linden walked past Blue and Kronch toward a large

green button secured under a plastic cover. Max and Ella watched him lift the cover, unable to believe their friend was about to have them turned into life-sized, sugary sweets. He looked across at them and smiled.

"It's for the best," he said, and lifting his hand he rested it on the button.

"Once Linden has started the machine," Blue began with an air of delight surrounding every sniveling part of him, "the conveyor belt will transport you under a delightful flow of choc-cookie mixture, before you're given a coating of warm toffee-caramel. You will then be covered in the multicolored sweetness of sprinkles. Soon after that, you will come face to face with the sharpened blades of the slicer, which will carve you up into tasty, bite-size mini-agents. That's my favorite part." He looked across at Linden who reflected an evil grin back. "You will have roughly two minutes to do all you'd like to do with the rest of your lives. Mind you," and at this he gloated even more, "in this position, your options are somewhat limited."

Ella remembered all the times she and Linden had e-mailed each other and spoken on the CTR. Her heart drooped as she watched one of the kindest, funniest people she'd ever met prepare to bring about her end.

"Linden!" she cried. "You aren't really going to do this, are you?"

He stared at her like he was in a trance.

Max looked up at the metal cauldrons and the shining

blades of the slicer waiting at attention for the order that would spell their doom. As much as she tried to deny it, Linden seemed to have been totally sucked in by Blue's cockamamie story about being the good guy. She looked at his blank face and struggled with the realization that she was being betrayed by the one person in her life she thought was her friend.

"Linden, what about our pact?" For one instant she thought she saw a hint of hesitation in his eyes, but it was no good. He pressed his hand down on the button and the conveyor belt jerked to life, beginning the process that would take Max, Ella, and Alex to their premature demise.

She frantically searched her mind for what they could do. When her backpack had been taken, she'd managed to sneakily grab a small satchel of sneeze powder. How could it be helpful?

Blue stared at his three bound prisoners like a hungry fox standing in front of a chicken coop.

"Bon voyage, ladies, and farewell to your last attempt at foiling my brilliant plans."

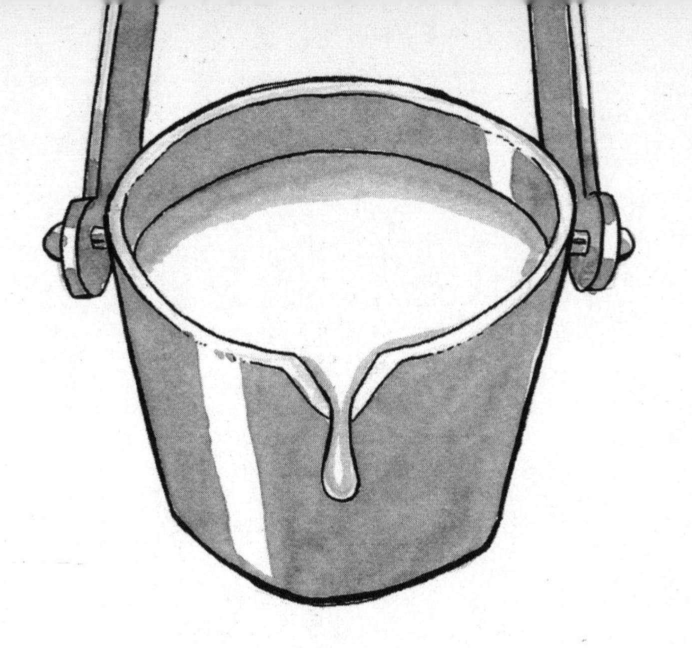

CHAPTER 20

Under the Moons of Mars

The clanging, whirring noise of the conveyor belt droned beneath Max, Ella, and Alex as it transported them toward the cauldrons of the Moons of Mars confectionery machine.

Max swallowed nervously and shifted inside the snug-fitting ropes as she got closer and closer to the tilting vessels and the best friend she'd ever had stood nearby and watched. Her stomach twisted into a ball of sadness and fear. She spoke to Alex.

"I liked what you said to Blue before. You really showed him," she stammered, still a little nervous about being so close to her hero.

Alex didn't reply. She was deep in thought, trying to figure out a way to save them.

"It was really brave of you to risk your life to find us." She blushed. "I always knew you would."

Alex looked around like she'd only just heard Max's voice. "Pardon?"

There was something about Alex's tone that made Max feel she had it all wrong. "It was good of you to try and save us," she tried again uneasily.

The glooping, oozing, sprinkling, and slicing got closer as the conveyor belt carried them ever more dangerously forward.

"I didn't come back to save you. I came to get the SAM so I could take the reading of the new ingredient to send to Spy Force. I'm on a mission to save the world, not

make new friends." And with that Alex went back to her thinking.

If Max felt sad before, she now felt as if her heart had been tipped over and emptied of all the happiness it ever had in it. Her Danger Meter was going crazy, while Blue, Kronch, and Linden blissfully lapped up the prospect of their imminent demise at the hands of Blue's Moons of Mars confectionery machine.

Ella hadn't heard what Alex had said to Max because she'd noticed something strange about Linden.

"Alex, Linden's eyes are a bit weird-looking."

Alex turned her head toward Linden and focused on his eyes. They looked glazed with a slight blue tinge.

"He's been given the secret ingredient," she surmised. "Blue instructed his technicians to make the side effects of the ingredient as minimal as possible, so they created a substance that is side-effect free except for a slight blue coloring to the eyes."

The sound of the slicer was getting louder and louder, like a hundred sharpened, plunging guillotines. But as they continued to look at Linden, another strange thing happened.

"Look," Ella gasped.

Linden was slowly reaching into his pocket.

"What's he going to do?" Max's eyes widened, thinking perhaps Linden's evil side had something else in store for them.

She looked over at Blue and Kronch. They hadn't noticed a thing. Blue's face was alight with a twitching, sickly smile and Kronch was indulging in a gross display of sniggering that was sending little balls of slobber spraying into the room. In fact, they were so preoccupied with the cookie-making process that neither of them saw Linden pull the Spy Force RHINO from his pocket. He kept his eyes firmly pinned on the machine, looking like he too was enjoying the show, while, barely moving, he aimed the device at a large cauldron above Blue's head labeled TOFFEE-CARAMEL.

"What's he doing?" Max was confused, unsure of who or what to trust anymore, including what she was seeing.

"He's directing the RHINO toward that cauldron," Ella said as they edged closer to the squirting choc-cookie mixture.

"And he's going to try and save us," Alex added without emotion.

Linden's eyes swept discreetly across to Max and sent her a small wink. For an instant she was bewildered about what it meant until she realized he needed her to distract Blue for the next part of his plan to work.

"Hey, Blue!" she shouted above the mechanical noise. "You're not as smart as you think you are, you know that?"

Slowly she slid her fingers into the pocket of her pink dress.

Blue gave her a quizzical look, which made him turn his back on Linden.

"Now, Maxine, what can possibly make you say that? I've had you tied up and placed on a conveyor belt where you have barely a minute left before you will be no more."

With his finger on the miniature joystick of the RHINO, Linden was maneuvering the cauldron so it tilted toward Blue's head.

"And what makes you think you're going to succeed?" Max asked, reaching for the sneeze powder and carefully taking it out of her pocket.

Blue let loose a laugh just as a clump of choc-cookie mixture blobbed right next to her ear.

"You're a feisty one, aren't you, Maxine? Even when you're beaten. I admire that in you."

"It's Max," she shot back, sick of people calling her that. "If you're as smart as you think you are," she challenged, seeing Linden's cauldron tip even further, "you'll look up right now."

Ella's eyes widened as a large blob of cookie mixture landed on Max's chest.

"Now, Max, what would I possibly want to look up for?"

"A final request?" she said sweetly, her Danger Meter vibrating so hard it was almost pounding through her rib cage.

"I guess it can't do any harm," Blue said. And as he did, the cauldron of gooey, toffee-caramel poured over him in one gluggy spurt.

His cries were muffled as he quickly became enveloped in the hardening mixture. He tried to pull it off but it stretched around him like gluey brown pieces of chewing gum. Kronch stood rooted in the same spot, as his pea-size brain grappled with what was happening, and just as he figured it out, Max hurled the bag of sneeze powder at him in a mini-explosion of white, nose-irritating dust.

"Ah-choo! Ah-choo! Ah-choo!" Kronch sneezed and, stumbling backward, bumping into machines, he landed headfirst in a fresh batch of toffee-caramel cookie goo.

Linden picked up a cookie mix bag and pulled it over Blue's head, causing him to fall in a sticky, mumbling heap. He then headed over to Ella and began untying her as another blob of mixture clomped on Max.

"Ah-choo! Ah-choo! Ah-choo!" Kronch continued to sneeze.

"What happened?" Ella wriggled in her loosening ropes. "I was worried that you really believed all that stuff you said before."

Linden untied the last of the knots and helped her off the moving belt. He then moved across to untie Alex.

"I didn't realize it at the time, but I'd been given a drink that had the secret ingredient in it. When it began wearing off, I figured out what was happening. Ah-choo!" Some of the sneeze powder had worked its way into Linden's nose.

"Mmmm mmmm mmm," Blue mmmed from inside his cookie mix bag as he spun around like a miniature tornado.

Linden struggled with the last of Alex's knots before he moved across to help Max.

"Ah-choo! Ah-choo! Ah-choo!" Kronch sneezed.

"When did it start to wear off?" Max flicked her head as the brown toffee goo began falling on her.

"Mmmm mmmm mmm," Blue mmmed and spun around some more.

"Around the time I took you to Blue's office." Linden's hands became covered with toffee-caramel as he tried to undo the last of Max's ropes.

"Ah-choo! Ah-choo! Ah-choo!"

There was a pause.

"Blue's office? Ah-choo!" Max had inhaled some of the powder as well.

"Yeah." Linden was almost through the ropes as another glob of toffee landed on both of them.

"You mean all the time we've been here, thinking we were going to die, you were pretending? Ah-choo!" Max could feel her temper rising.

Linden realized that his plan, which had saved their lives, may not have sounded too good.

"I can't believe you'd do that!"

"Ah-choo! Ah-choo! Ah-choo!" Kronch's sneezing attack continued as he bumped into Blue who mmmed like he was in pain.

Max was totally covered by toffee caramel as the sprinkles made their way toward her.

"It was the only way I could get close enough to you to try and save you. Ah-choo!" he explained.

"Wait until I get off here. Ah-choo!" Max warned, the sprinkling process falling on her like colored snow.

"Do you want to be freed or not?" Linden asked, a little of the evil-inducing ingredient making him unusually impatient with Max.

Ella noticed the blades of the slicer getting closer and closer.

"Maybe you two should talk about this later?" she suggested anxiously.

"Ah-choo! Ah-choo! Ah-choo!" Kronch sneezed as he stumbled into a bag of flour, which powdered over everyone.

"No. I'd like to talk about it now," Max insisted, before sneezing again.

"Mmmm mmmm mmm," Blue mmmed again from inside his cookie mix bag.

"Max!" Alex shouted.

"And another thing—" Max began.

"Max! The blades!" Ella cried.

Max looked up and saw shafts of glistening steel fall just inches in front of her face. The next slice was meant for her. Just before they fell, Linden lunged forward and, grabbing her arms, dragged her off the conveyor belt and onto the floor.

"Ah-choo!" Max and Linden sneezed together.

Ella and Alex breathed a deep sigh of relief as the Moons of Mars confectionery machine continued to whir on as if nothing had happened.

CHAPTER 21

Back at Spy Force

Max, Linden, and Ella stood in front of Harrison's desk holding fresh tropical juices Steinberger had made them. Actually, Ella and Linden were holding theirs while Max's drink perched on a high stool near her face with a long straw in it because the Moons of Mars toffee mixture made it hard for her to move.

They each sipped and watched as Steinberger tried to help Harrison unhook his sling from a rack of fishing lines he'd become entangled in. He was wearing a sling because of an accident he'd had that morning, during a meeting with the Brazilian foreign minister, when he was reaching for a rare and unique garden gnome that was sitting a little too high on the mantelpiece. He stretched up to the gnome, grabbed its foot, but unable to get a proper hold, stumbled backward. He only just managed to catch the gnome with one hand as the other became twisted behind a marble carving of himself that was given to him as a present from the people of the Congo—when it used to be known as the Congo.

If Max could have moved or made any facial gestures, she'd have firmly folded her arms across her chest and scowled at having spent the entire journey from Blue's Foods to Spy Force bent into Sleek's sidecar, while Linden and Ella chatted incessantly like a pair of parrots at sunset. They were all full of themselves as they talked about the mission and, what was even more disgusting, Linden was saying some of it in French, which he'd started studying at school after Ella had told him she'd lived in Paris as a kid.

Blah blah blah, they went on and on. *Ooh-la-la and big deal*, thought Max. She was still angry with Linden for lying to her during the mission and making her feel as if he'd turned his back on her. She'd never felt so alone in her whole life, and here he was laughing and talking to Ella like it was nothing.

Finally, after a tricky struggle, Steinberger freed Harrison from the fishing rods and left him to make his way to his seat behind his desk.

"Team," he said importantly, straightening his tie with his one good arm. "Well run . . . I mean, well *done*. On behalf of Spy Force I'd like to thank you for helping uncover the evil plans of Blue. Linden, the drink sample you brought back for us to test was put through the SAM and came up exactly as we thought. The special forces have been sent in and we hope to have Blue behind bars, where he belongs."

Ella sent Linden a warm smile that Max would have called "soppy" if anyone had asked her. Which they didn't.

"Awesome! Ah-choo!" Linden still had traces of sneeze powder in his system.

"Oh, and Max?"

Max's heart tripped over itself.

"Yes?" she asked eagerly, hoping perhaps he had something special to tell her.

"Sorry there isn't time to let you get cleaned up, but Sleek has got the plane fired up and you know how he is about keeping on schedule."

"That's okay," she lied, thinking her journey home couldn't be any more uncomfortable. She was still wearing that stupid pink dress while the other two stood around in their own clothes.

"Spy Force is so proud of you three and would like to take this opportunity to officially declare Mission Blue's Foods a success."

Harrison held his juice aloft as Steinberger pressed the *play* button on the tape machine and a chorus of celebration music sounded throughout the room. He then burst into an impulsive and hearty round of applause. Ella and Linden clinked their glasses together while Max sucked on her straw and felt an itch on her nose start up.

But that wasn't the only thing bugging her.

"Mr. Harrison? Where's Alex?"

"Alex doesn't like to hang around for the festivities. Never has. She's an elusive one, our Alex."

Max tried not to sound obvious. "Did she leave any messages?"

"Once a mission is finished, she just takes off. She's not too fond of good-byes."

Max was disappointed. She knew that she and Alex hadn't got along too well, but she was sure they'd be great friends if they got to hang out a little more.

For now, though, there was something else she had to tell Harrison.

"There's one more thing I need to tell you about the mission, sir. One of your Spy Force officers is a double agent."

Linden and Ella looked at each other.

Harrison's face clouded over.

"Tell us what you blow . . . That is, what you *know*."

Max knew what she had to say was going to shock everyone, and she could hardly wait to tell them.

"It's Dretch."

Steinberger frowned.

"I thought we'd been through this already, Max. Dretch is one of our most loyal members and has been with the Force since its inception."

Harrison took the accusation very seriously.

"Let her speak, Steinberger. Tell us how you know this, Max." Harrison put his sling on the table and prepared to listen.

"When we arrived, he made it clear that he didn't like us and warned us that we may not make it out of Spy Force alive. And his cat, Delilah, is his spy. Turning up to gather information just when it is needed. Dretch always flinched when he heard your name, and he snuck into the lab and tampered with my laser so that it failed during the mission."

Steinberger and Harrison exchanged a solemn look.

"Steinberger. Ask Dretch to come in, will you?"

The tall, lanky man did as he was asked. Max stood by and contemplated how proud Harrison would be of her now that the mission was completed and she was about to uncover a double agent.

"You have made a very grave accusation, Max." Harrison's voice was low and measured. "Let's hope you're not jumping to conclusions."

"I have no doubt, sir." But hearing the tone of Harrison's voice made Max's certainty falter.

Within a few short minutes Dretch was standing among them.

"Max tells us you might be a double agent," Harrison got straight to the point.

Dretch spun his head toward Max so fast that she stepped back.

"Did she now?" His voice was full of anger. "And what makes her think that?"

"Max? I think it's best if it comes from you at this point," Harrison invited.

Max swallowed to moisten her suddenly dry throat.

"Every time Harrison's name was mentioned to you, you'd flinch, almost as if in disgust."

Dretch dug his hands deep into his pockets.

"I never knew it was a crime to feel loyalty toward someone. We've worked on many missions together, and Harrison always thought about others before himself. It will take my whole life to repay the kindness this man has shown."

Max swallowed again.

"And what about you sneaking into the lab just before we got our packs and my laser not working when I tried to use it during the mission?"

Dretch fixed her with a iron stare.

"Quimby asked me to fix some equipment of hers. She was present every second I was there and can vouch for everything I did."

"And what about the threat you made to me about not making it out of here alive?"

Max suddenly became more confident, remembering the venom in his deadly warning.

"I think it's dangerous to have kids working on missions when they aren't trained and can't make proper judgments. I was just letting you know that what you were stepping into wasn't fairyland but real and dangerous work."

If Harrison wasn't present, Max was convinced Dretch would have jumped across the room and flattened her toffee-coated body into a million sweetened pieces.

"I'm sorry for the interruption, Dretch. You can go back to what you were doing."

Max felt about two inches tall.

Harrison fixed her with a stern eye.

"Max, what just happened must never happen again.

It's pleasing to see you are keeping so aware of your surroundings, but a good agent is sure of all the facts. Dretch is as fine and loyal an agent as any I've met. In fact during our last mission together, he saved my wife . . . I mean, *life*."

A tear pricked the corner of Max's eye as she realized she'd gone from hero to sugarcoated idiot in the space of about ten minutes.

Beep, beep, beep, beep!

Steinberger looked at his beeper.

"It's Sleek. Time to go."

Harrison beamed at all three of them. "Your mission is done, and I'm proud of all three of you. Until bedtime. We'll be in fudge," he said before wincing and correcting himself. "I mean, until *next time*. We'll be in *touch*. *Au revoir*."

On their way to the terra-cotta ride, Max lagged a little behind the others as she struggled with her extra sweet, toughened layer and her sadness at disappointing Harrison. As she turned a corner toward the elevator, she ran headlong into the sallow features of Dretch.

"I told you to keep out of my way," he sneered.

"I . . . I . . ." Max stammered as the others moved ahead.

"I'm not interested in excuses, and if you ever try to muddy my name again, you might just find yourself adrift in some gooey mess you won't be able to get out of so easily. Just stay away from me, got that?"

He disappeared as Steinberger reached the elevator and turned around to see how she was doing.

"You okay, Max?" he asked jovially.

"Sure," she answered, again feeling the icy chill customary upon meeting Dretch. She'd really earned his anger in Harrison's office, and now he hated her even more, but there was something in her that knew he wasn't telling the whole truth and she was sure going to keep an eye on him next time they met.

After a brief terra-cotta ride, they arrived at the VART, where Sleek had the jet ready and waiting.

Steinberger walked a little slower to stay with a slow-moving Max. He thanked them a million times for their work and recounted over and over again how successful the mission was and what it meant for the world. He told her not to feel bad about Dretch. He was a good guy, not the easiest to get along with, but he wouldn't hold any grudges about her mistaken conclusion. He spoke so fast it was a wonder his lips could keep up. What he said made her feel better, but suddenly Max wasn't worried about his lips or what he was saying or about Dretch; she was more concerned about trying to overhear what Linden and Ella were whispering about in front of her.

She missed most of it and what she did hear was all in French.

Why did she spend most of her life looking silly and feeling as if she were the odd one out?

When they reached the end of the ramp, it was time for Ella and Steinberger to say good-bye. Sleek, as usual, had the invisible jet prepared for takeoff.

"There's a jet there?" Ella exclaimed.

"Sure is, and you should see it inside," Linden answered.

The engine blasted an eager jet thrust.

"Maybe next time." Steinberger was well aware of Sleek's need to keep on schedule.

"Max?" Linden asked, hoping she'd get the hint and move away so he could say a quiet good-bye to Ella.

"Yes?" she said innocently, knowing full well what he wanted.

"Maybe you should get on the jet first. Make yourself comfortable," he suggested.

"No, I'll wait for you," she offered kindly, not wanting to leave them alone for a second.

All four of them stood in heavy silence as Sleek climbed out of the cabin.

"Everyone ready?" he asked. Then, seeing Max's sweetened layer, he broke off a piece of toffee and plonked it in his mouth. "We leave in one minute."

Linden and Ella tried to cover their smiles as Sleek climbed back in the jet.

"'Bye, Ella. I'll call you when we get back home."

"That'd be great. 'Bye, Max."

"'Bye," Max mumbled.

Steinberger hurried them along. "Sleek has been

known to leave without any passengers," he warned.

"'Bye, Mr. Steinberger. Thanks. For everything," Max managed through toffee-stiff lips.

Max followed Linden as he climbed into the jet and found his seat. As they buckled up, the hatch closed and they waved good-bye.

"We did it," said Linden warmly.

Max tried to smile.

"Yeah, we did," she said feeling a little better as the invisible jet taxied out of the VART and carried them away from their first successfully completed Spy Force mission.

CHAPTER 22

Au Revoir, Mindawarra

"When were you working for Spy Force?" Max and Linden had arrived back on the farm and, after a very long bath that dissolved her toffee coating, Max was now sitting at the table facing Ben and Eleanor over banana sandwiches and orange juice.

"Most of the time we were in London," Ben said matter-of-factly, taking another bite out of his sandwich. "In fact, once you've been inducted, you're members for life, but I guess Harrison told you that. They've got great fringe benefit offers, too."

"Why didn't you tell me?"

"They're a secret organization, Max, you know that. We can't tell anyone."

"Even me?"

"Even you," Ben said, taking a slurp of juice as if he were telling just another everyday story.

Eleanor leaned across and held Max's hand. "We knew you'd been recruited and that you'd gone to London to be inducted into the Force. We got an e-mail from Spy Force before you left. They are a world-class operation and take very good care of their spies. It's a good career. As long as in your everyday life you act just like any other kid. We're so happy for you."

This was so bizarre. Ben and Eleanor not only knew about their London mission—minus the details, of course—they were once spies themselves. A few times they were involved in missions, but mostly they worked in the labs.

"Does Mom know?"

"No," Eleanor answered gently, trying to soothe Max's shock.

"Another sandwich?" Ben asked, reaching for his third.

"No, thanks. I think I might just go to bed."

It was the last day of Max's visit to the farm, and she was waiting in the front room for her mother. She hadn't seen much of Linden over the last few days because he was busy helping his father—and also because she was doing her best to avoid him since she was still upset with him for lying to her during the mission.

And for liking Ella more than her.

Trouble was, as she rested her chin on her arms and stared out the window, feeling small in the long, sinking sofa, she missed Linden and was feeling sad that he hadn't come to say good-bye. She heard the back door slam and Eleanor's voice drifted down the hall.

"She's in the living room packed and ready to break our hearts."

There was a short moment where Max heard nothing before she turned to see Linden standing next to her.

"How do you do that?" she asked.

"Do what?" he frowned.

"Just turn up behind people?"

"Not sure. I guess it's the angelic side of me kicking in before its time."

Max didn't smile.

"Can I sit with you until your mom comes?" he asked.

She moved to the end of the sofa, leaving him heaps of room to sit down, then she stared at the carpet in front of her.

There was this annoying silence that sat between them like a stranger.

"Ella called."

Just the name made Max clench her fingers.

"She said Blue's Foods is being shut down and there are TV reports that a big Japanese firm is going to buy the company and keep making all the favorite foods as they were originally."

Max pretended not to be too interested but was hanging on Linden's every word.

"By the time the police reached the factory," he continued, "all the evidence had been destroyed and Blue had disappeared, leaving no trace that he was even connected to the company except for his name."

"They didn't lock him up?"

"Nope. Couldn't find a trace of him."

"That means it won't be long until he plans another scheme."

"Yeah," Linden agreed, happy Max had started to talk to him.

There was another one of those long silences. Max had so much she wanted to say to Linden but nothing would come out.

"Max," Linden began uneasily. "I know you're still mad at me for what I did at Blue's factory, but I was only doing what I thought was best."

Max didn't budge. Sometimes she could be so stubborn Linden was sure if he looked up the word in the dictionary it would say, "See *Max*."

"Besides. We did it. Our first official Spy Force mission."

No response.

"And I still think we make the best team there is."

Max smiled reluctantly.

"If you hadn't understood why I'd winked at you, we'd all have been in big trouble," he said. And, dropping his head a little, he added, "And I would have lost a really good friend."

Max smiled even more as she tried to find the words to tell Linden the reason she was angry was because she thought he didn't care.

"It's just that—" she was interrupted by the crunch of gravel beneath tires, as her mother's car drove toward the house.

Great, thought Max. *When I want her to arrive, she doesn't, and when I want her to stay away, she's here.*

"That's my ride back to paradise," she joked.

Linden smiled. "When are you coming back?"

"Not sure," she answered, feeling as if she wanted to say something nice but couldn't think what. "Maybe you could come and visit me in the city."

Linden's face turned into one of those big smiles that took over his whole body.

"That'd be great! You could show me all your favorite places."

The car pulled up in front of the house.

"Yeah," Max said, walking over to pick up her bags.

Linden got up off the sofa and pushed a strand of hair out of his eyes, but just as quickly it flung back.

"It's good to see you're back to your normal self." Max never thought she'd be so happy to see his uncontrollable hair. "I got worried, too, that you really meant all those things back there."

"I might think you're a bit difficult at times, but not enough to want to turn you into a giant cookie."

Max smiled. Linden really did have a way of making things seem okay again.

She heard a car door slam and looked out the window.

"Oh, no," she moaned. "She's brought the kid with her."

"Who?" But before he needed an answer, Linden remembered. "Aidan. Let's watch," he said, jumping onto the sofa and thinking this should be fun.

"Yeah," Max gasped excitedly, preparing to watch another awkward family reunion.

After a quick check in the mirror and applying more lipstick and other face goo, Max's mom got out of the car, straightened her tight skirt, and adjusted her overdone salon hair. The kind where they spend hours making it look like you spent no time on it at all. She giggled and preened herself as Eleanor and Ben said hello and shook hands with Aidan. Ben was holding a well-behaved Ralph on a leash but when Aidan stepped closer, Ben had to hold him back.

Grrrrr, Ralph growled.

"Ralph," Eleanor scolded, "you don't do that to guests."

Ralph quieted down, but they could tell he didn't like Aidan and was only being good for Eleanor.

Aidan nervously stepped around Ralph and plastered on one of those Hollywood grins that was so fake it looked like he'd been practicing it in front of the mirror for weeks.

Again Eleanor did her best to invite them in, but after a short desperate look from her mother, Aidan made some smarmy excuse that was so slick Max could just picture them rehearsing the answer in the car. Then there was silence, since they could think of nothing else to say.

"Another famous family moment," said Max.

"These hellos and good-byes are fun," Linden cracked. "But then I always have a good time when you're around."

Max blushed. "Thanks," she said quietly, feeling the same. "I—"

"Max, honey? It's time to go, sweetie." Her mother's timing was terrible as usual.

"That's our cue." Max got off the sofa and picked up her bags.

Outside there was a stilted series of hellos and "darling" pecks on the cheek.

Ben kept a tight hold of Ralph and looked at Max.

"He promised he'd be good this time."

Ralph sat up even taller just to prove it. Max had to admit that was cute.

"Thanks for everything. Can I come back soon?"

"Any time you like." Eleanor folded her up in a big bear-like hug as Max's mother looked on, a hint of jealousy on her face as the hug continued a little longer than she thought necessary.

Ben handed Ralph's leash to Eleanor and gave Max a hug that was just as warm.

"Don't take too long about it, that's all," he said, and he scooped her up and twirled her around like she was a rag doll. Max giggled as the farm dipped around her feet.

All the hugging and twirling made Max's mother uncomfortable, and she tried to hurry things along.

"We should be going." Her smile was a mix of anxiety and muscles trying to keep up a fake smile.

Max turned to Linden. "See ya."

"See ya. We'll do it all again soon." And with that he winked.

Max laughed. "Yeah, let's do that."

Max's mother looked at Aidan, smiling an apology at how long this was taking.

Ben and Linden packed Max's bags in the trunk and Max opened the back door of the car. Just as she was about to climb in, a crescendo of screeching and a flurry of feathers and dirt burst in front of her. She lost her balance and toppled onto the ground.

Geraldine. Max should have known she wouldn't get away without a good-bye from her.

"You'll get yours," she warned the chicken as it innocently strutted away.

Eleanor lunged toward Max and helped her up.

"I'm so sorry, Max. Geraldine's normally so quiet. Are you okay?"

Max's mother stood nearby watching Eleanor fuss. She moved in before Max had a chance to say anything and took her out of Eleanor's arms.

"Of course she is. Aren't you, sweetie? No use fussing, you're still alive and we're late." She brushed Max down and just as quickly stepped around to the driver's side and got in the car.

"Thanks, Eleanor. I'm fine," Max whispered to her aunt, the person she'd miss more than anyone.

Max climbed into the back seat and Ben closed the door after her. Then Max, her mother, and Aidan took off in a storm of dust in her mother's hurry to get back to the city.

"Yeah. We'll do it again," said Max. She leaned her head against the window. She was Max Remy, Superspy, and she was going to be back.